Be Your Own Salmon

An Allegory with 25 Lessons for Swimming Upstream in the Wild River of Life

Thomas S. Dittmar
with Roger S. Peterson

Jessica - Swim on & on & always
Be your own salmon!!
Thomas S Dittmar

Be Your Own Salmon: An Allegory with 25 Lessons for Swimming Upstream in the Wild River of Life

Published by Wheatmark®
1760 East River Road, Suite 145
Tucson, Arizona 85718
United States of America
www.wheatmark.com

ISBN: 978-1-62787-060-3 (paperback)
ISBN: 978-1-62787-061-0 (ebook)
LCCN: 2014934017

rev201401

Dedication

Be Your Own Salmon is dedicated to my first son, James Thomas Dittmar.

It was truly an honor to be the father of James. Born August 8, 1989.

He was the first of my two sons. I watched and loved him from a small preemie baby, to a young towheaded boy with an ever present smile. Then the middle years, having the best times camping and fishing with his brother Michael and me. Time flew by and he became a strong, proud, handsome young teen.

That's when I started writing *Be Your Own Salmon*. I wanted it to be a guide to help him get through life a little easier and maybe avoid some of the troubles and hardships that I and others had experienced. To be a guide for rest of his long, fulfilled lifetime, a guide for his children, and theirs.

For some unknown reason, it was not to happen.

James died in a car accident at age twenty-one on October 15, 2010.

His loss has been the most heartbreaking thing ever, not just for me, but also for my ex-wife, Kendra, his brother, Michael, his friends, and extended families. The pain and feeling of loss cannot even be described.

To say that he was loved and is missed by many, would be a monumental understatement.

God bless you James, until we fish again in heaven. This book is dedicated in memory of you. Your loving father.

Thomas S. Dittmar

Contents

Preface ... vii

I Got the Idea Along a Wild River ... ix

1 Young Smolts . . . Young Smolts ... 1

2 Is This the Way Home? ... 14

3 No Fish Down There! ... 22

4 The Perfect Cast? ... 28

5 One Last Cast ... 34

6 Who Caught Whom? ... 39

7 Who's There? ... 50

8 Fish Eye View ... 59

9 Back to School ... 73

10 Playing Hooky? 85

11 A Blind Salmon? 95

12 Shiny Rocks! 114

13 Foot by Foot up Lilliput Trail 125

14 Final Test . . . Promise Kept 137

15 Self-Discovery 149

Epilogue 169

Preface

The story in *Be Your Own Salmon* is for people who are stuck and don't know what to do next. Stuck professionally. Stuck in the Great Recession. Stuck in menial jobs right out of college and swimming in student debt. Stuck in that teenage belief that life will be instantly wonderful on one's eighteenth birthday, or graduation from high school. Stuck in the fear that no one will hire a stay-at-home mom once she is ready to return to the workforce. Or a middle aged man, going back to school to start a new career.

It is for someone who is suffering from the loss of a loved one and who doesn't know how to move forward.

The wisdom of the book is in its characters. Sal and Master Cohosaki show Deyoung Smolts, a young father and automobile salesman who is failing at sales and stuck in his life, how to get unstuck . . . and succeed at sales and be a top performer! Not just in sales, but in life!

This is a book for anyone in need of sage advice to regain control of his or her life. In these hard times, is that you?

The little story inside these pages can adapt to whatever difficulty you seek to overcome. You will dive into the wild river of life with Sal and learn how to swim upstream.

My teenage sons, James and Michael, and the many salespeople

I have trained and wish to train in the future were originally my target audience. But since finishing the book, I know many people will benefit from the wisdom of the salmon.

I have held many positions in the automobile business, from salesman to general sales manager. For more than thirty years I have gathered the knowledge to fill these pages.

This book is about swimming out of the muck of excuses and taking charge of your life. Here you can learn about yourself, maybe even relearn who you once were, and discover who you can be . . . with a little help from Sal, Deyoung, and Master Cohosaki.

Yoga practitioners may see the eight steps of yoga in *Be Your Own Salmon*. After all, yoga is about living life, and so is this book. But here you will also find the Twenty-Five Lessons of the Salmon. These are life lessons, universal to all, so please take time to read these twenty-five lessons. Mark them with a highlighter, or write them down on a sheet of paper. Upon finishing the book, you will see if your wisdom matches that of Sal, king of the king salmon.

To get you started, here is one of the lessons. But you will have to find it in the book to figure out its meaning *for you:* "Be the message that you send."

I Got the Idea Along a Wild River

The idea for *Be Your Own Salmon* began to gel when I was a young boy. My father, John Dittmar, was stationed in Thailand during the Vietnam War. My mom, Fusako; my sisters, Patricia, Jeanette, and Irene; my brother, John; and I were living close to the American River in Rancho Cordova, California near Sacramento.

My best friend, Philip Green, and I would ride our bikes down a winding dirt path to the river. We would fish and swim and play along the banks. In the fall, we noticed the salmon running upstream. We wondered how they did that. I became intrigued with the wonders and power of the river and the size and beauty of the salmon that swam it.

Avid fishermen will find in this story added magic and meaning to their favorite pastime. I will never forget the look on my mother's face when I brought home the first salmon I caught and how proud I was to have done so.

During my early teens, we lived in Germany for several years, but we eventually returned to Sacramento. My high school friend Randy Cole introduced me to Lilliput Trail and the greatness of the Yuba River. We spent many unforgettable years fishing and gold prospecting in this history-rich California mother lode. My love of wild rivers grew stronger.

In my late teens, I reunited with Philip. We were soon good friends again, and we decided to be roommates. Phil, our friend Bryan Jackson, and I shared his old childhood house next to the river, leaving me with happy memories of summer parties and rafting on the river, including one trip at night under a full moon. But those memories include sadness and loss. Philip's death in an auto accident made me realize the value and preciousness of life and the finality of death. Our time together on the river became part of how I viewed the river of life.

At first I wanted to become a graphic artist, but I soon found myself selling cars at a local Ford dealership. I became top salesperson within my first year and assistant manager within three years. But along the way I also experienced my share of failure. Such is the life of a salesman. During this time I married Kendra. We soon had two beautiful boys, James and Michael.

So I stayed in the car business, working for Elk Grove Ford Chrysler Jeep. I made a ten-year run from assistant sales manager to finance manager to sales manager, and then I hit my big goal: general sales manager. In the early '90s, I started writing a column in the monthly dealership newsletter on the importance of keeping a positive attitude. But I never knew if anyone really cared about the articles.

After the dealership group dissolved, I later had a chance meeting with Brian Clark, the dealership's fleet manager. He told me, "Tom, thanks for writing those articles . . . and I really liked the one about *being your own salmon*." He recalled how that one article had inspired him to forge ahead whenever times were tough. I was surprised yet grateful that something I had written years ago could still influence someone's life.

That was the inspiration to start writing *Be Your Own Salmon* as a book. But after years of starts and stops, nothing was coming together on paper. It seemed like the book would never get written.

As luck would have it, I had an encounter with Joan Waters, a local magazine editor. After briefly describing Deyoung, Sal, and Master Cohosaki, the characters you will meet in this book, I found her speechless. Her husband, too, just sat silently. They were both staring at me. Suddenly she pointed her finger at me and said, "You *have* to write that book! You're going to be on Oprah Winfrey's show!" I looked at her husband, and he was nodding in agreement. I was humbled and thankful for her journalistic nudge.

That night I told my wife about Joan's encouragement. We promptly went out and bought me a laptop, and I started writing *Be Your Own Salmon*.

With encouragement from many people, such as my ex-wife, Kendra, my whole family, especially my sister Trisha, my best friends Randy Cole and George Perez, Bill "the Good News Newsman" Bailey for his professional encouragement, my first editor, Mary Gardner, and special thanks to Roger S. Peterson, my main editor. His professional backing gave me the push I needed to get this project upstream.

Everyone's help was greatly appreciated. Although I was able to finish the book, the euphoria of writing it came to a sudden halt.

The events in the years 2010 and 2011 were going to prove to be my greatest life challenge.

It started with the passing of two friends, one of them a great childhood friend, Bryan Jackson.

A filing of personal Bankruptcy.

The economy taking a huge blow, and devastating the auto sales business.

Then the tragic and sudden, unforeseeable death of my first son, James.

A divorce that ended my twenty-five-year marriage.

My second son, Michael, rupturing his colon and enduring a twelve-hour life saving operation.

Then me getting not one, but two, life threatening MRSA staff infections.

Yes, all in a two-year period!

I was dropped to my knees, and then some.

But I got up. I swam on.

I now realize that *Be Your Own Salmon* is not only the sales guide that I first intended to write, but also a life guide, not just for the people who read it, but for me.

It's a guide to help me try to understand what happened, and to move forward despite it.

A guide to help me live out the rest of my life, to swim on, as . . . the salmon I am.

My wish is it does the same for you, or maybe for someone you know.

Thank you,

Thomas S. Dittmar

1

Young Smolts . . . Young Smolts

I stared out the window, daydreaming, my fingers gently rubbing the beautiful gold and quartz nugget that hung from the chain around my neck. "I wouldn't sell this thing for ten thousand dollars," I said to myself as I noticed a yellow and black finch dart across the skyline.

The sight of the bird brought me back to reality, and I began to ponder the day ahead.

It's going to be a typical Northern California summer day. The forecast called for 100-plus degrees. Am I ready? Let's see. Healthy breakfast. A power walk with King, my dog. Two pens. Sunblock. Light-colored cotton shirt and pants. Lightweight shoes. Jug of ice water. Three appointments . . . and a positive attitude. I remembered the old adage, "A salmon that fails to plan for what's ahead is the salmon that normally ends up dead." A telling smile crossed my face. *Okay . . . should be a great day.*

"Young Smolts . . . young Smolts," I heard faintly. "Young Smolts," the voice repeated.

"That's Deyoung Smolts!" I abruptly declared, as I snapped out of my daydream and looked up from my chair. I glanced around. My fellow car salesmen and managers were staring at me and breaking out in laughter, and I suddenly remembered that I was in the first-of-the-month sales meeting. *Oops,* I thought.

I quickly regained my composure, rose up out of my chair, and made my way to the front of the room. George was yelling at me to wake up. Jeff shouted something rude. I ignored him. Steve, the finance director, gave me a high five as I passed by and quietly joked about borrowing a couple hundred. Randall and the others clapped and then slowly began to quiet down. Slightly embarrassed, I worked my way through the rows of salesmen who sat in front of me and walked up to meet the general sales manager, Pete Salcedo.

"Deyoung Smolts, Top Salesperson, June 1986," read the plaque.

"Deyoung, that's five out of six months now," Pete said as he reached for my extended hand. "Congratulations!" He briskly shook my hand and smiled. Reaching into his pocket, he pulled out a wad of money and started to count. "One, two, three, four, five, six, seven," he counted slowly, the salespeople joining in as he stacked hundred dollar bills on the table. "Eight, nine, ten. That's one thousand dollars!" he exclaimed as he picked the money off the table and handed it to me.

Applause rang out as I accepted my bonus and humbly shook Pete's hand. "Thank you, Pete," I answered. Another round of applause followed.

My team members, George Perez and Randy Morse, were clapping but still laughing at me, having caught me in a daydream.

I gratefully thanked everyone again as I folded the cash in half and quietly slipped it into my left pocket. With my free hand, I gave a last wave of thanks for the kind applause. I turned back toward my seat and thought to myself, *No bragging for me. Not my style. Humble pie is a good pie; that's a fact.*

Sitting down, I put my elbows on the table, rested my chin against my hands, and smiled. *Yes, life is good. Life is good.*

As the meeting ended and the room cleared, I glanced up and noticed Pete motioning to me. Knowing I could not say no, he asked, "Deyoung, do you have a minute?"

"Uh, nice working with you, Smolts," George said jokingly when he overheard Pete ask me to stay and talk.

I smiled. Of course, since I had just received the Top Salesman Award and no one from human resources was around, I felt pretty comfortable taking this meeting. I brushed off George as he exited the room and turned to Pete. "Yeah, Pete. What's up?"

"Hey, have a seat," answered Pete. He motioned to the nearest chair. "I just wanted to ask you a question."

"Sure. Uh, no problem," I said with a quizzical look on my face.

"Deyoung," he said, "now, ah, you have been pretty quiet the last nine months or so, but you keep winning Salesman of the Month. If my memory serves me correctly, the only time you *didn't* win Salesman of the Month, you took your wife to Hawaii for a week on the trip you were awarded for winning top sales for the prior month. And I think you still almost won that month, even though you only worked three weeks!" he said with a proud smile.

"Now, I've asked you this before, and all you keep saying is, 'Keeping my nose upstream, keeping a positive attitude, giving a hundred percent every day, swimming in the clean water,' or something like that. And you keep rubbing that gold nugget and making funny sounds. What's the deal there? You know, I'm getting tired of that corny answer you have been giving me and everybody else. Deyoung, I'm sensing something more here. So, what have you been doing?" he pressed on in a demanding, but friendly, manner.

I dodged the question. "Not too much."

"Don't give me that baloney," he said. "I have been around too long now. What are you doing?"

"Nothing different," I said, as I tried in desperation to hide my secret by avoiding direct eye contact with him and turning away.

"Don't give me that," Pete persisted, and he shifted his body while trying in vain to look me in the eyes. "Ever since last October you've been a selling machine! Plus, I rarely see you on the sales floor looking for customers because you have tons of appointments. And when you're with a client you seem to have all the answers—and they want to buy from you. Plus, you have a great gross profit average and a great customer satisfaction rating. Then there is the fact that we offered you a position as an assistant sales manager and you turned it down because you were making more money then they do and working fewer hours!"

The desperation in his voice made me turn to him. He noticed and focused right into my eyes, "Now, what are you doing?"

"Really, Pete, just keeping my nose upstream and—"

"Deyoung . . . stop! What are you doing? I need to know," Pete said in a tone that left me no choice but to answer.

"Just being my own salmon," I mumbled, barely audibly. I was determined not to tell him, but I found myself saying, "You wouldn't believe me anyway."

"Believe what?" He quickly shot back. "And did you say *salmon*?"

"Uh . . . nothing," I said.

"No, believe what?" Pete persisted with the closing skill of a thirty-year auto sales veteran.

Pete sensed I was cornered. He had seen his opening, and he was going for it. My once-strong defense was beginning to crumble. I began to cave. "Okay!" I suddenly blurted out. "I am being my own salmon," I answered confidently.

"Being your own salmon?" he said, utterly confused.

"Yes. Being my own salmon. Pete, I'm glad you're sitting down, because you may not believe me. It all started about ten months ago," I began. "Something happened to me. Something really strange, and so . . . so surreal. I haven't told anyone about it, not even my wife."

Pete sat down next to me, his attention now fully captured, and asked, "What was it?"

"I can't tell you," I stammered, even though I knew my defenses were fading fast.

"You have to tell me, Deyoung; I *need* to know!" he pleaded.

"Okay, Pete. I am going to trust you with this. But, please—it doesn't leave this room," I pleaded as I glanced toward the closed door.

"Fair enough," Pete said. He settled in his chair and gave me his promise and full attention.

"Pete," I started with as strong a tone as I could muster. "I am not kidding around. You're either in the water or on dry land."

"What?" Pete answered in confusion. "In the water—"

I abruptly stopped him cold. "Uh, I mean you're either with me on this or not. We shake hands and you give me your word. No one else hears this story," I reiterated in the strongest tone my dry mouth could muster.

"Deyoung, I give you my word," Pete said as he extended his hand. We shook, and the warmth and sincerity of his handshake settled me down a little.

"Okay. Here goes," I replied as I reluctantly began to tell my story. "Well, Pete, it was October 8th of last year, and I came in for my morning shift. At first it seemed like any other shift, but then strange things started to happen. I'll just start at the beginning."

IT WAS COLD, WET, AND freezing that day. My nice dress shoes were soaked through, and my socks needed ringing out. They were wet from stepping in the puddles formed between the endless rows of cars we had to unlock that morning. Take the key off the board, put it on the car, unlock the car, and pick up the keys—350 cars later we were done.

My hands? Almost thawed. My hair? Almost dry. My sport

coat? Don't ask. The coffee? Doing me no good. I could barely feel my legs and feet.

Okay, I have to get pumped up! I thought. *I have been here an hour already, hiding in my cubicle. I need to sell a car . . . today! I better go stand out on the point and get an "up"—or a "fresh customer," as our boss wants us to call them. Let's see. Where is my pen? I need a pen and I need a deal. It is the eighth of the month and I have no sales. Everyone is riding my butt and asking me what's happened. What do they mean? I am the same person I was when I started here at American River Auto Sales six months ago. Funny, it feels more like two years. I started out so great. What* did *happen? Well, can't worry. Got to get a deal.*

Standing up, I headed for the front door. Dawn, the receptionist, gave me a funny look. My waterlogged shoes squashed rhythmically as I walked by. "Catch a lunker," she said.

"Thanks," I responded. I burst through the front door before I realized what she had said. *Catch a lunker? What did she mean by that?*

Walking out the front showroom door, I headed for the huddle of salesmen standing under the gazebo. The gazebo was where all the salespeople hung out. We would call the colors of cars, guessing if they might turn in to the dealership. If you spotted a car and called it first, you got to help them if they turned in. That was our "up."

Seeing the salesman huddled in the distance, I thought, *Well, let's see. One, two, three . . . eight, nine, ten, eleven. Man! There are at least a dozen salespeople out here already. How am I going to get an up, much less a deal? This should be fun . . . not!*

I gathered my energy and geared up for the dash through the rain for the protection of the small gazebo. *Okay, go!* I jumped over the curb and set out in a fast walk. The stinging cold rain on my cheeks reminded me I needed an umbrella, but I had left it at home. I crossed the pavement over to the huddled mass.

"Up blue! Up blue!" Someone yelled.

"Late!" I yelled as I jumped into the wild fray.

"You called nothing!" barked George, who we sometimes called Jorge just for fun.

"Yeah, you're late," confirmed Kevin "K-Dog" Martin.

"Smolts!" yelled Jeff. "Don't try to steal our ups, dude."

"Shut up, Jeff!" I shot back. Man, I hated that guy, always getting on my nerves and throwing me under the bus. "I think he is half responsible for my bad luck of late," I muttered to myself.

"Okay, maybe I missed it," I shot back in a defensive tone. "Get the next one, Smolts," I said to myself. I stood there a while. *Nothing's coming.*

Paul, who talked in a slow Alabama drawl, suddenly turned to me and nodded his head. "S'up, Smolts?"

Before I could answer, he followed with, "Man, it sure is slow today. This rain stinks, huh, dude?"

"Yeah, it's cold out here, man." I tried to stay warm in my soaked sport coat.

"Man, no good ups coming in either," Dan said.

"I'm going to get one!" I said to him. I tried to see over the taller Keith Pope. "Hey, Pope, move over, dude," I asked him, knowing he would not budge from the prized spot he had claimed.

I started to think that there were too many people out here to get an up. *And the only luck I've had recently is bad luck. What's my problem?*

"Up blue!" *Nothing.* "Up silver! Up white! Up! Up!" *Nothing. Maybe Dan was right.* "Up! Up!" I yelled out. Was I ever going to get an up?

After a half an hour of calling out, I called a fresh one. "Up red!" I looked around—no one offered any resistance. All right: my turn now. "What do we have here?" I said as I examined my opportunity.

Damn. The vehicle veered toward parts and service. Great. Probably just here for service. The red sedan pulled into the customer parking lot near the parts department. "Damn it!" I said, as I watched a single woman and no one else get out of the vehicle. How many am I going to get this month? No husband or dad to help her. She probably just wants parts anyway.

"Here for parts?" I asked the young lady as she stepped out of the car. She looked up at me with a somewhat startled gaze.

"Well, yes," she said, "I would like—"

"Great!" I cut her off. *Just what I thought—parts department,* I pompously confirmed to myself.

"It's right over there," I said with a patronizing voice. "The big blue door on the right side. Sign says Parts Department." I then reached into my pocket for my cigarettes. *Time for a smoke break. I have been out here too long and it's cold,* I thought to myself.

"Uh, thanks," the lady replied. She turned and walked away as fast as she could.

It's cold. She probably just wants to get in and out. Just my luck anyway. Another parts customer. Even if she is looking for a car, I bet she has bad credit anyway.

I searched my pockets for my lighter and found it inside my jacket. I pulled it out and fumbled with the safety. *Fricking great, Deyoung, running between the raindrops is what I'm doing. Everyone is selling cars and making money and I can't get a break.* I walked toward the smoking area, disgusted with my bad luck. After a twenty-minute smoke break, I prepared to go back out to the point.

About forty-five minutes later, I heard a booming voice. "Deyoung, what the heck are you doing?"

"What?" I smashed my third cigarette out in the ashtray and turned toward the voice. *Oh, shoot! My boss, J. J. Jones.* "Uh, yeah, J. J., I was just with some lady. Sent her to parts and I needed a break."

"Needed a break," he answered back coolly. "A little tired, are you?"

I did not like the way this was sounding. "Well, I better go get an up," I said. I tried to slink away.

"Not so fast," he quickly snapped, forcing me to turn and face him. "Rick Painter has a write-up with the lady you lot-dropped earlier."

"What?" I answered back with a puzzled and defensive tone.

"Yeah, it seems that after she visited the parts department, she walked into the showroom and asked for a salesman. Well Painter was right there and now has her landed on a new Camaro, and they are close to a deal!"

Keeping my defenses up as best I could, I shot back, "Well, she was here for parts . . . and besides, she probably won't qualify anyway."

That was not what J. J. wanted to hear. "Well, let me tell you, Deyoung, I recognize her from my bank," he shot back angrily. "She's the bank assistant manager!" he said with a red face. "Do you even have her name and number?" Knowing I did not, I fumbled in my shirt pocket, pulling out my business card follow-up system. "Doesn't look like it," I said.

"That's just great," he barked. "Painter is on another crew, so we will both get no commission when she buys. You and I are going to have a talk," he stated. "And a serious one. In fact, follow me right now and—"

All of a sudden the loud speaker blared overhead, "J. J. Jones to the sales tower. J. J. Jones to the sales tower . . . one-O."

"Damn, gotta go," J. J. said, his voice trailing off. The urgent page had distracted him.

Whew, lucky me. Saved by the intercom, I thought to myself.

"Don't think I'm done with you, Deyoung. We will talk!" J. J. declared strongly. He turned toward the sales tower, his pace picking up at the urgency of the "One-O" code for "get over here as soon as possible."

I left the smoking area and meandered sheepishly back toward the huddle. *Great,* I thought, *no car sales. My boss is totally ticked off at me. I have no appointments and no money made. Last month I had to go into my savings account just to pay bills. What am I going to do?*

Suddenly, the intercom blared, "Go fishing, Smolts. Go fishing."

What was that? I looked around. No one else seemed to have heard it. I asked K-Dog as he strolled by. "Hey bud, you hear that, man?"

"Hear what, bro?" he asked in a smooth low tone.

"Dude, the intercom, a second ago. It announced, 'Go fishing'—or something like that."

"Fishin' . . . whaddayamean, fishin'? Man, I didn't hear jack on the intercom. You spun or somethin'?" he fired off as his arm flung high in the air and he walked away.

Okay, this is too weird, I thought. *"Go fishing"? I haven't gone fishing in years. I glanced about for a likely prankster. No one around—probably one of the guys playing a joke on me,* I figured.

Wanting to see if J. J. was just jiving me about the lady, I walked up to George, who was standing by the key-box. I blurted out, "Hey, Jorge, you think Painter has anything?"

George looked straight at me. "Dude, you freakin' blew it. That lady owes nothing on her trade and she is preapproved at her bank. They just closed a four-pounder on her—*that's four thousand dollars that you won't be getting twenty-five percent of.* What were you thinking? Did you turn her when she came in?" he asked.

"Oh, shoot. I thought she just wanted the parts department," I said defensively.

"Well, she wanted more than that," George stated. "You lost out, man."

I stared blankly out toward the street, pondering my bad luck. Then I heard the intercom again. "Go fishing, Smolts."

"George, did you hear that?" I asked him in urgency. "Are you messing with me?"

George stared blankly at me. "What the heck you talkin' about, man?"

"Did you hear 'go fishing' on the intercom? Did you hear that?" I asked, my voice crying out for any acknowledgement of the unusual voice.

George looked at me again. "Deyoung, are you going nuts? What are you smoking out there?" he laughed. "Yeah, go fishing, you idiot. In fact, catch the world-record salmon. Make a million dollars," he joked. Then his face straightened out. "Seriously, dude, you better get your act together, or they're going to blow you out. And you better get a car deal before J. J. finds you. I am going back to the huddle, and you should, too," he said firmly.

I just stared at him, startled at his bluntness. He seemed ready to say something else, but he turned as if disgusted by my actions and briskly walked away.

Great, I thought. *No deal for me. Even my good bud George is grinding me, and . . . and now I'm hearing things.* I headed back inside to the safety of the showroom and my cubicle. I hopped the curb and swung open the huge glass door.

As I walked through the door, I glanced to my left. No one was at the phone desk. It occurred to me that I could man the phones for a while and maybe get a phone pop. I took a seat at the desk and stared at the phone. My stomach growled. *Where's that roach coach food wagon when you need it?*

I began to think back to my first days at the car lot. It had been only six months since I started. Man, I had started out great! Seemed like everyone wanted to buy from me. I was the next superstar, they said.

Deyoung Smolts . . . top salesperson. Man, that sounded good. And I almost got it my second month. Ed Dansby, the "ol' warhorse," beat me out on the last day of the month. Three people came in and bought the last day. The lucky son of a gun. I grimaced thinking how close I had come.

Then, out of the blue, I started to think about fishing. I hadn't been salmon fishing in six, maybe seven years. It used to be one of my favorite things to do with my dad. Why had I stopped? I thought about what George said: a million dollars for a world-record salmon catch. *Well, it's probably not a million, but it's sure to be worth enough money for me to pay some bills.*

I had been getting pretty good at fishing, and I'd caught some nice fish, too. But I had been too busy of late to do any serious fishing. Besides, this job was taking too much of my time, along with my wife and my young boys, James and Michael. There was no time to go fishing. Plus, with my luck lately, I probably couldn't catch a cold, much less a record-breaking salmon.

Ring, ring! Ring, ring! The phone startled me back from daydreaming. "Hello, this is Deyoung Smolts, how can I help you today? Hello . . . *Hellooow*?"

"Go fishing, Smolts," the voice said, just like the one I had heard over the intercom.

I froze for a split second. "That's it!" I yelled. "Who's messing with me?" I wheeled around and slammed the phone down. No one bothered to look at me.

I'm okay, I thought. Someone is just screwing with me." I quickly dialed the store operator.

"Dawn, who just called in on that last sales call?" I blurted out.

"No one has called in a while, silly," she coldly stated.

"What do you mean? I just had a sales call. And, I—"

Click went the receiver, as she punched another line.

Ohhh . . . I am not feeling well, I thought. "Joy, will you watch the phones for a while? I don't feel well."

"No problem. You okay?" she asked in a caring tone.

"Oh, I'm okay," I lied. "I just need to take a rest."

"You going for a coffee or anything?" she inquired.

"No, I think I should go sit down for a while . . . or go fishing."

"What?" she asked.

Uh, nothing," I said as I walked off. I headed toward my cubicle and sat down at my desk bewildered by what had taken place. *I am going nuts.* Something made me glance at my watch. *It's three o'clock already. How did the shift end so quickly?* Well, I wasn't going to argue about how or why. I was going to get the heck out of there.

I grabbed my still-soaked coat and headed for the door. *Don't look around, don't look back.* I didn't want anyone to stop me for a lecture.

"I'm out of here!" I yelled to Dawn.

"Good luck," she said.

"Thanks," I said without hesitation.

'Good luck'? Why did she say that? I thought as I burst through the side door out to employee parking. I walked quickly toward my car. I noticed the skies clearing and decided my soggy coat would be best in the trunk instead of on the cloth seats. Fumbling for the trunk key, I found it, popped open the trunk, and glanced inside.

"Whoooaa! What's going on?" I said as I spotted fishing gear inside. *How the heck did that stuff get in here?* I stood there dumbfounded, and then I quickly threw my coat over the pole, creel, and vest as if covering evidence of some kind of wrongdoing.

"Too weird. I haven't seen that stuff in a while. I bet Kendra put it in there. Probably wanted to get it out of the garage," I mumbled aloud. I slammed the trunk lid and jumped in. I started the car, revving up the motor before turning off the wipers I had left on during the morning's rain. I glanced up at the clouds. The sun suddenly burst through a small opening, basking my car in brilliant light.

2

Is This the Way Home?

I pulled my car onto J Street and turned east onto Highway 50 toward home. I popped a CD into the player and turned the music up loud. "These mist-colored mountains are all right for meeeee," I sang along loudly as I sailed down the freeway.

I drove without thinking. The farther from the car lot I drove, the lighter the rain became until I had totally escaped the early autumn storm. It seemed the storm cell settled over the city, but only scattered clouds dotted the foothills surrounding it. Suddenly, a passing road sign caught my attention. "Discovery Park—Next Exit."

Discovery Park? I thought. *That's the opposite direction from home! What the heck am I doing on this freeway? Hey, wait a minute. That's near where I used to live and go fishing when I was a boy. Hey, this is where I used to live as a kid! What am I doing out this way?*

Almost on instinct, I turned my car off the freeway, as the decision to go fishing seemed to be more destiny now than thought. This "go fishing" thing was really starting to get to me. I did have my rod and reel, and it looked like my waders and gear were also in the trunk. There was no harm in stopping.

If only I had a fishing license, I thought.

But then I noticed a tag hanging from my rearview mirror. It was a fishing license with my name on it.

No! That was not there a minute ago! my mind yelled.

I started to get goose bumps. In my bewilderment, the license began to swing back and forth like a pendulum from the car's motion down the winding road. I hadn't had a license in six or seven years.

The hypnotic swinging of the license calmed me down as I wondered if Kendra had put it there too. *Well, you can't fish without a license, so it's a good thing it's there.*

"Okay, Deyoung, just go with this," I said to myself.

I snapped to and grabbed the license and its lanyard off the mirror. I figured it had been too bad a day for me not to enjoy myself for a couple hours with some peaceful fishing. I turned down familiar streets as childhood memories raced through my head. Turning onto Coloma and then left on Rossmoor Drive, I followed the road through the neighborhood until there it was: my old house, right on the corner. A flood of emotions surged through my body as I stopped in front. The small pine tree in the front yard looked much taller now. I remembered hopping the curb with my bike and my front tire falling off midwheelie, sending me flying over the handlebars onto the grassy front lawn.

I smiled, as I remember the look on my mom's face, when I dragged an old salmon home I had caught at the river. Thinking that must have been the start of my love for fishing for the beautiful fish.

The house was a different color now, I noticed, but the memories continued to flow. I remembered soaring on the swing out back with my sister, Jeanette, sing about rocket ships. I remembered playing with my old childhood friend, Philip, who used to live just down the street. Sadly, I remembered his passing away in a tragic car accident years later. A quick glance at his old house down the street, was a quick reminder of where he used to live.

If I continued going straight, I figured I would end up on that old dirt road that took me down to the river in my younger days. I took one last glance at the house and moved onward, knowing that time wasn't on my side if I wanted to do any fishing today. Still, the house's image lingered in my head as I rolled through the stop sign and continued to the waiting river that lay a quarter-mile or so down the road.

As I drove down the winding road toward the river, more memories raced through my mind. It had been years, but it looked so familiar.

This road was special, those times were special. The wonder years, riding the dirt road on my bicycle with my fishing pole swinging from my handlebars, grinning from ear to ear. It was a dirt before, but now it was covered with smooth black asphalt. The smooth S curves looked familiar. But they were now lined with four-by-four posts run with thick cable that stopped only when I came upon signs warning of the fifteen mile per hour speed limit and the upcoming bike paths. The familiar piles of dredge tailing unevenly lined the road, and they were no longer covered with fresh spring grass, obviously the result of the oncoming winter.

I began to remember the towering oaks, the roar of the river, and the smell of the air. I missed it here. I loved the history of this area. The California Gold Rush started right in this area. Sutter's Fort and the Marshall Gold Discovery site were not that far away. I had always wanted to go gold prospecting, but I had never had the time.

"Maybe one day," I said aloud.

I continued until I reached the parking area on the right. It did not look the same as the big dirt patch in my memories. Now it was paved and had a restroom, and a single lamppost stood sentry over a lone trash can. *The restroom may come in handy.* I pulled in and noticed the typical smattering of vehicles, 59 Chevy fleetside, an old four door Malibu with more Bondo than paint, a nice red 69 Mach 1, and an old orange Pinto. *Fishermen's vehicles.*

I quickly stopped as a man and woman raced by on fancy bikes, oblivious to me with their headphone-covered ears. I noticed big mounds of river rock with grazed tops of hand-sized cobblestone. The mounds surrounding the parking lot had patches of dying weeds stuffed in the crevices.

"Nice spot to catch grasshoppers if I were trout fishing," I said to myself.

Pulling into the nearest parking spot, I rested for a minute and glanced toward the river. I could barely see her as I peeked out the windshield to get a better look over the dunes and brush that lay between us. *There she is. Whew awesome!* I remembered the recent passing storm cells and noted that she was running a little high.

"Let's see what we got here." I said as I stepped out of the car.

The air smelled fabulous. I took a big deep breath, glanced up at the rustling trees, and headed for the back of the car. "Where are my damn cigarettes? Gotta have a smoke," I muttered. "They were right here." I patted my pockets. Cursing my luck for not finding them, I fumbled for the trunk key, opened the trunk, and saw my sport coat lying over the tackle. I reached down to remove it. As I tossed it aside, I began to take inventory: Neoprene waders, fishing vest, two-piece fiberglass rod, heavy-duty open-face spin-cast reel, thirty-pound super strength mono, sweatshirt, and creel.

"Well, I've got everything I need," I said, assuring myself. "Man, where did all this stuff come from?" I asked aloud.

The only explanation was that my wife must have put it in there. *Who else? Should I call her and let her know where I am?* I continued to sort out the gear. Pulling out the waders, I glanced around to make sure no one got a free peep show as I changed into them. I quickly slipped off my shoes and work pants. I wondered how cold the water was going to be.

No worry, I thought. *Neoprene waders are like magic out in the water. No cold feet for me!*

The waders were a little large, making it easy to slide my right foot into one of the legs. As I lifted my left leg, I temporarily lost my balance, causing me to hop out from behind the car door on one foot as a boy and his dog walked nearby. The boy was seven years old or so, with glasses and dark hair. He appeared to be part Asian. He was not startled at all, just stood tall and looked at me with eyes that seemed to stare right through me. He had the oddest sense of familiarity.

"Going fishing, mister?" the boy asked.

"Uh, yes, I am." I pulled the final boot over my socks.

"Watcha fishing for?" he questioned.

"Salmon," I proudly said. "King salmon."

"That sounds like fun! You know the path?"

"Yes, it should be fun." I smiled, and then I stopped. "Um, do I know the path?" I had just caught what he said.

"Yeah, you know the path," he restated in a matter-of-fact voice.

"Path?" I questioned again.

He made a small but distinct nod to his left, not adding a word. I turned to see what he was looking at and noticed an old path on the downstream side of the river.

"Oh, no. I'm fishing with that group over there." I gestured toward the huddle of fishermen nearby. "That's where everyone fishes. Hey, nice beagle."

"Thanks, mister," he replied.

"What's her name?"

"Penny," he answered happily.

A chill shot through my spine. "Wow, now that's a coincidence. I used to have a beagle named Penny when I was a kid."

The boy smiled again with that same sense of knowing.

I bent back into the trunk to grab my hat and turned to ask, "Hey do you live around—"

He was gone. *That's strange. Where the heck did he go?* I looked left and right and around the car. *Gone . . . just like that. Wow.*

"Just a strange day, Deyoung," I said to myself as I finished pulling on the waders. *Oh, well, no big deal.* I blew off the encounter. *Gotta get fishing!*

I ducked back under the trunk hood and noticed that the safety belt for the waders stuck on the creel as I lifted it out of the trunk. It would keep the water out of my waders if I happened to fall while wading in deep water. *No need for that,* I thought. I never waded out over my waist anyway. I grabbed it and tossed it back. I threw on my hat, put on my fishing vest, slammed the trunk closed, and turned toward the river. *Okay, I'm going fishing!*

Two paths lay before me. The path that led straight over to the other fishermen was less of a path and more of a line of cobble-sized rocks littered with fishermen's cans, broken beer bottles, and fast-food packaging. The fishermen, standing side by side, didn't really look like they were having much luck. It all suddenly reminded me of the huddle of salesmen at work, calling out colors and ups.

The path to the left, the one the kid had pointed out, was a sandy path that led through the weeds. It almost invited me to enter into the thick underbrush of oak, cottonwood, and thick blackberry bushes that lined the river's edge. Yellow finches darted in and out of the shade cast by the massive oaks. The breeze picked up, causing a small shower of leaves to fall around me.

"You know the path." *What was that kid talking about?* Something made me glance left again, and I noticed an opening in the leafy blackberry bushes that were the main player in the thicket that lines the riverbanks. *Funny,* I thought. *No good fishing spots are down there. I don't even remember a path that way.* Of course, it had been a while. Besides, I was going to fish where all the other guys were fishing.

I stubbornly chose to trudge over the rocky, garbage-strewn terrain toward the other fishermen. But it seemed the distance between me and the fishermen stayed the same as I walked and walked. I lifted my foot to step over a small boulder and caught my toe on the edge and tumbled toward the ground. I winced at the inevitable impact. The ground raced toward me. I threw out my left hand to soften the shock, while my right hand waved wildly in a heroic attempt to save the fishing pole.

Wump would best describe the sound I made as I fell onto the trashy trail below. I was stunned but happy to have saved my pole. My first thought was to jump up as quickly as possible to avoid the embarrassment of falling in front of my fellow fishermen. No luck. With the breath slightly knocked out of me, I lay there. I tried to yell for help from the other fishermen, but no sound came out of my mouth. It seemed the fishermen were turned away toward the river and didn't even note my presence.

As I lay there stunned and helpless, the only thing I could see was the opening to the path on the left that the boy had pointed out. Not knowing what to do—and I could do nothing—I pondered my fate as memories of the small boy and his words swept through my mind. "You know the path," he had said. I continued to stare at the opening of the new path. A warm feeling rushed through my body as my mind leaned toward taking the new, cleaner path. I noticed the beauty and serenity reflected in it. Slowly, I realized I could move my hands, and then my arms, and eventually my whole body began to recover. In all this elation and new energy, I found myself saying, "Take the new path!"

"Okay, now get up, Deyoung! You've got some fishing to do," I told myself. Slowly, I braced my hands on the rough sand. I pushed and rose to one knee, then the other. I knelt there for a moment as if frozen in prayer.

"Please, let this be a good fishing day," I said instinctively, as a sudden burst of sunlight showered down upon me. I instinctively glanced up, then I winced for a second and adjusted my boonie hat to shield the sun's rays from my eyes. I took a breath of clean, fresh air and slowly rose to my feet. I stood there for a moment like a statue, basking in the sun's warmth. Then I took a second deep breath, turned, and walked toward the new path.

3

No Fish Down There!

I gathered myself together and approached this new path, not knowing what to expect, but somehow sensing I was headed in the right direction.

As I walked, I heard the fisherman start to yell to me in an uneven cackle—so they *did* notice me!

"There are no fish down in that part of the river. Hey, young man—no fish down there!" they yelled, but I continued walking away from them.

The shouting faded as I forged ahead and slowly disappeared into the dense, prickly foliage. I struggled to keep my rod tip pointing straight down the path to avoid breaking it. My cotton sleeves and dangling creel dodged the gauntlet of wild thorny blackberry bushes that lined the path. I was careful not to stumble over the sand, roots, and rocks that lay below me. The path was rough, yet the foliage seemed manicured. I was careful where I walked, as if not to disturb a garden.

I noticed that a flock of wild turkeys had gathered to my right. The large male leading the group noticed me at the same time and shooed his harem along. I could see a deer in the distance. Birds were fluttering around in the canopy above. The amazing sounds, the fresh aromas, and the visual majesty captured my attention as I wandered aimlessly through a place I did not know.

After what seemed like a long walk, the path began to clear. In the distance, I noticed a freshly formed sandbar. It rose gracefully, like a deserted island from the depths of the ocean. It framed a large cove that looked like a good place to fish. I surveyed the trail in front of me for the easiest access.

The rough trail had gradually turned to soft sand that gave way beneath my feet. I made slow progress toward my newly discovered fishing spot. Soon the trail cleared, and I saw a chance to duck through some bushes and cut over to a small clearing. From there it was a straight shot over to the sandbar.

Grabbing a branch with my free hand to maintain my balance, I worked my way over some rocks and small boulders. The boots of my waders slipped into a small pool of brackish water as I briefly stumbled.

"Be careful, Deyoung," I mumbled. "Just a little while ago you were headed home, and now you are risking your life walking along the river with no one in sight. Not real smart." I quickly caught my balance and broke through the over-growth.

"There she is. And what a marvelous sandbar it is!" I whispered.

As I waded to the tip of the sandbar, the sounds of the river grew louder. The constant droning of the water overpowered most of the other sounds that dared to challenge its authority. I marveled at the beauty that surrounded me. Large sycamore, oak, and dogwood trees lined the river and were in full autumn fashion. The sand was soft as sand should be and strewn with small pebbles and driftwood. A bright yellow finch with jet-black markings landed on a twig that protruded out of a large bush. "The bird was just like the ones I fed daily at home. *A good omen"*

I quickly looked about for a spot on the beach to set up. A

small rock looked like an inviting place to sit as I gingerly set my pole down and slid the creel off of my shoulder.

I thought again how glad I was to be here at this moment. As my eyes wandered the landscape, a leaf fluttered down from the sky and landed on the rippling water. It swiftly took off down-river. *The end or beginning of its journey?* I thought as I watched it disappear, realizing I was taking the time to watch nature in motion as never before.

I surveyed my surroundings further. Every good fisherman knows it's important to look around before he fishes and to carefully assess the landscape for danger spots and escape routes. I had always made it a habit to do this, because one never knows if a fish is going to make a run, and you might have to run with it.

I straightened up as my eyes followed the shoreline about seventy yards to where the smooth sand gradually transformed into muddy shoreline. *Trouble,* I thought.

I spotted a large jumble of driftwood and shrubs lodged in the branches of a tree that had fallen into the water. The trunk formed a bridge from the bank to midstream, where it disappeared into the swift moving river. "Gotta stay clear of that," I warned myself, knowing the log and the debris caught in its branches would act as snag line for anything that floated by.

The left side of the river was relatively clear. If I wanted to go farther down the left bank and avoid the trees and bushes, I would have to cross a large back-eddy that had formed below the sandbar.

Between the glare of the setting sun and the rippling water, it was hard to tell how deep the eddy was. I figured it was about three, maybe four feet deep. It should be fine if I had to cross it, I surmised.

The view was fairly clear across the river. The bank was steeper and more prone to clearing from high runoff. I determined it was too far across for me to be concerned.

I examined the condition of the water. The water looked high and fast upstream. I saw the white-capped water churning and gurgling as the river burst unevenly over the rocks and boulders that dared reach above the water line.

Wuuump! Splash! I instantly knew the sound. Salmon. I spotted a large fish rise and dive about forty yards off to my right. I saw another one to my left. This was a hot spot, all right!

The water ran unrelentingly over a small but steep waterfall that dropped into a pool formed at the bottom. The water slowed there. Every once in a while I could see a salmon take off and shoot up the fall, struggling to get to the level above.

I glanced to the left, temporarily blinded from the silvery reflection shining off of the water as it flowed downstream. With the clouds from the storm clearing in the distance, it was going to be a fantastic sunset.

"It must be about four o'clock," I figured, giving me about two hours. "Okay, survey's over. Danger right. Left is okay, but watch out for the cove," I told myself as I wrapped up my checklist.

"Now, time to settle down and fish," I said to myself. I took a deep breath of pure river air. "Ahhh, it has been too, too long."

I slowly lowered my body into a sitting position and set the fishing pole gently to my side. Time to see what kind of fishing gear I had with me. I picked up the creel and reached for the opening. It felt heavy as I flipped open the snap. I reached in deep. *Nothing?*

"Where is my box of jigs and flatfish?" I could not believe I hadn't checked. *Oh my gosh,* I thought as I peered into the empty bag. I reached in again and felt something. As I fingered the bottom of the bag, I slowly lifted out my safety belt. "How the heck did that get in there?" I asked aloud in confusion, certain that I had left it in the trunk. More importantly, there wasn't a lure in sight.

I took another look inside the bag. Empty. *Nothing to fish with!*

How stupid of me not to have checked earlier at the car, I steamed as my blood pressure rose and I festered over my predicament.

Suddenly a bright silver flash briefly blinded me. Something was hanging from the safety belt. A lure! And a nice one. I reached for the dangling little jewel. It looked like the custom-made lures my Grandpa Tak used to make. The large spinner had a wire body with crystal beads, stacked white and red. A sterling silver spoon was attached with a stainless steel loop and a large stainless steel treble hook, sharpened to the finest points. *Saved.*

"Nice," I said as I turned the lure over in my hands. I noticed the red dot on the silver spoon. "Yes! It is Grandpa Tak's!" I shouted with satisfaction. *But how did one of Grandpa's old lures get on this safety belt?* I wondered as I twisted it off the vest and stared at it.

My Grandpa Tak was a legend in his own time as he trolled the Sacramento River back in his day, my mom had told me. I remembered watching him make these lures, marveling at the pure silver and shiny beads. I reflected back to the few times I was able to fish with him. Then a splash shook me out of my temporary trance and I looked around for a safe spot to place the lure. I gently laid it on a flat river rock.

I reached for my long fiberglass pole, focusing in on where the reel connected to the rod. I wrapped my pointer finger through the top of the reel and the others through the bottom. I held the rod straight out in front of me and relished in the power I felt as I gently lifted the tip toward the sky. *Line ready to go. Nice action and firmness,* I thought. *Just need a little weight.*

I reached instinctively into the upper third pocket of my vest for a sliding sinker. I held it in my palm and shook it like dice. With my thumb and pointer finger, I held it up to the sun. Perfect weight. Stainless steel. No lead to harm my river. I carefully threaded it onto the line. I figured about three feet below the lure would be good as I reached into the lower pocket on the right side of the vest and pulled out a small split-shot and crimped it onto the line with my teeth.

Perfect, I thought as my hand moved toward a small pocket on the sleeve of my vest. *Gold swivel and I am ready to go.* I grabbed the swivel and tied it onto the tip of the line using an old fisherman's knot. I secured the final loop and yanked it tight. Grabbing the small scissors hanging from a line attached to my vest, I carefully trimmed away the excess line while being careful to stash it away for proper disposal. Holding the swivel, I snapped it open as I fastened the final assembly, the lure. *And not just any lure,* I thought. *Quite possibly the last remaining Grandpa Tak lure in the world.*

I delicately grabbed the lure off its temporary altar and slipped it onto the gold swivel, locking it securely into place. I let it dangle in the setting sunlight, shimmering and glistening as it spun around.

"Well, let's give it a shot," I muttered softly to myself as I turned toward the churning water.

4

The Perfect Cast?

I held the rod firmly in my right hand and waded a couple feet out from the shore. I was scouting for a good place to make the first cast. Below the small waterfall, the water slowed and formed a deep pool. I figured that for a likely spot. I would need to be careful and not throw the lure into the falls and risk losing it by snagging it in the rocks and boulders.

I went through my mental checklist. After gauging the wind direction, I hand tested the drag strength of the line with my fingers, adjusted it, and flipped over the bail that secured the line in place, then I let out about two feet of line and held it firmly with my finger. The lure swung back and forth in the breeze, the silver spoon shining brightly as it spun freely. Everything looked good.

I made one last survey of the water and planted my feet in the loose gravel.

"Okay, Deyoung, make her a good one," I said to myself as I reeled back with my right arm. The rod responded, arching back in a graceful bow, ready to spring forward and deliver the lure to the sweet spot. With one smooth motion, I whipped my arm forward and released my finger from the line to free Grandpa's lure into flight.

The lure arched high into the sky as the line spun smoothly

from the reel. "Perfect!" I said, as the shining lure rainbowed toward the center of the river. It's a sight a fisherman never tires of seeing.

"Just the right spot!" I congratulated myself as the lure hit the water about twenty feet below the waterfall with that delicate little splash I love to hear.

Okay, now let some line out and find the bottom, I thought to myself, slowly letting the line run through my fingers. The line stopped for just a second. I quickly flipped the bail to set the line in place. The sinker should be sitting on the bottom, and the lure should be about five feet downstream from it.

I waited in anticipation of a possible strike. *Maybe I can get lucky today and catch that record salmon,* I let myself think. *No way. Too much bad luck at the dealership lately even to think about catching a big fish,* I countered, figuring my luck ran in a pattern.

I stood there for a moment, my feet firmly planted in the loose gravel. I began to enjoy the peaceful seclusion of my newly found special, secret fishing spot. But soon my mind wandered. "What am I doing here? How did I end up fishing?" I asked myself with growing puzzlement.

A sudden stiff breeze snapped me out of my temporary trance. Figuring I could use a little extra help after a minute of no action, I decided it was time for the old fisherman's call.

"Heeeeere fishy, fishy . . . heeeeere fishy, fishy. Here fishy, fisheeee," I called aloud in a high-pitched voice. A weak smile crossed my face as memories flashed by from the times my dad and I had used that old call. We would laugh at how silly it sounded but at the same time marvel in the luck we had over the years using it. I repeated it again. "Heeeeere fishy, fishy. Here fishy, fisheeeeeeee!"

My fingers felt a small tug on the line. "What was that?" I asked. My body and mind were at full attention now as I slowly raised the rod up and looked toward the tip.

Tap, tap, the rod tip went. I tensed up my forearms in anticipation of a hard strike. "Okay, Deyoung, watch the line now, watch the line. Don't blow it," I warned myself. "Don't jump the gun."

Again, *tap, tap,* then *bam!* The line shot straight down and took off. I knew it was a big hit. I waited for the right moment to set the hook. "Okay, wait, wait, wait . . . now!" I shouted as I pulled back the rod.

"Yes! Fish on!" I burst. "And a nice one!" The line held firm and created the perfect union between the bowing rod, the line, and its wild fleeing foe. It's a thrill unmatched by any other.

"Okay! Fish on, baby. Fish on!" I yelled out into the cool evening air.

In an instant, the line took off to the left, peeling yards off the reel at a quick pace. The drag was set lightly in case of a snag.

Whizzzzzz! The reel screamed as the fish took off, obviously not happy about his dinner turning into a fight for his life.

"This seems like a nice fish!" I said. As I scrambled to my right, then left, I almost lost my balance slipping on a mossy rock that lay right below the waterline near the shore. I held the rod tip high with my right hand to keep tension on the line while adjusting the drag with my left. With the gracefulness of a ballerina—*if I do say myself*—I twirled toward the safer footing of the sandbar and scrambled to the shore. The day was turning out great after all.

"Oh, no . . . you're not getting away!" I shouted while adjusting the tension on the line. As I made my way toward the tip of the sandbar, I wondered how big the fish was and, more importantly, which way he was going to run.

As I reached the end of the sandbar, the fish's twisting and turning made it hard to gauge his size. I determined this was a good place to make my stand and to figure a way to land my catch.

The fish swam toward me, jolting me to reel in my line. It

turned upstream, perhaps realizing it was nearing the shore. I kept my rod high over my head and followed the fish up the shoreline.

Perfect spot to play a fish, I thought as I scrambled up the sandy bar. The line stretched to the point of putting pressure on the drag, so I let it out a bit.

Oh, it feels pretty heavy, I thought with glee. I contemplated tightening the drag some more. I kept the rod pressure strong, but then I felt the fish weaken to the point that it seemed the line tension might be getting too much for him to handle. I glanced downstream toward the setting sun. Still time, I determined. I lifted the rod higher to increase the pressure on the fish and reeled faster. The fish was about forty feet away and was getting tired. So was I. My arms ached from the unexpected workout.

"Time to land this baby!" I looked around for the right spot. *Finally! Some good luck, Deyoung,* I allowed myself to think as I walked carefully out several feet into the water to greet the fish. I slowly pulled my prize into a shallow area and stared intently into the crystal clear water.

The glint of the sun on the rippling water made focusing difficult. I peered into the depths for my prize.

"What the heck?" My eyes focused on the fish. "A carp. A carp!" I could not believe my eyes as I watched this trash fish struggling in the slow current. I was torn between disbelief and total frustration. This was so typical of how my luck was going. I pulled the carp toward shore and saw that it had some weeds hanging from it. I realized that was the reason it had seemed so heavy. It was really only about a five-pounder. "Dammit!" I looked up toward the sky, shaking my head. "Is this what I came out here for?" I shouted out loud in a "why me" cry.

"A junk fish!" I repeated. I could hear and see salmon jumping in the distance. They seemed to be mocking my lack of fishing prowess.

I reached into the large pocket of my vest and pulled out my pliers to extract my valuable lure from the carp. I gingerly set the pole down, then I reached for the fish's gills and pulled him up to the shore.

I reached down roughly and grabbed the dangling lure with the pliers. *Man, it's in there good.* I struggled to remove the hook from the writhing fish. "Dammit!" I screamed as the hook bent sideways as I hurried to remove it. "Arggh!" I yelled from deep in my lungs. "Now I only have two good hooks on my treble hook! The bent one looks like it's ready to break." The lure finally worked free and fell to the sand.

"That's it! You have ruined my day!" I yelled at the carp. "Now you are going to get yours!" And, in almost blind hysteria, I reached for my knife in preparation for the rightful execution that justice required.

I fumbled with the snap on the sheath and flipped it open, exposing the handle of the knife. Gripping it firmly with my right hand, I slid it out, exposing the deadly blade. I held the now barely breathing fish with my free hand. "Prepare to die!" I said with a Darth Vader-like voice.

I raised my hand to plunge the knife into the fish. But the splash of a salmon jumping nearby stole my attention. At that moment, I heard my dad's voice, "You're going to eat it, aren't you?"

"What?" I asked to nothing but air. The knife was poised in midstrike. "What was that?" I asked. "Am I going to eat what?" I asked again. Looking down, I caught the eye of the carp. It stared at me in total submission. "I'm not eating no carp!" I said as my eyes turned away from the fish in a flash of guilt and remorse.

"Deyoung, it's the rule of the land: you kill it, you eat it," I could hear my dad say. I remembered him saying that many times when we kids were camping.

With fishing, it's "catch and release." We did occasionally eat a trout if we killed one by a bad hook set.

He wouldn't let us shoot any live creatures with our BB guns unless we were going to eat them. He had once made my brother John cook up a small bird he had shot and eat some. It wasn't a pretty sight. I remembered him getting sick afterward and swearing never to kill anything on purpose again, unless it was for food.

And yet, here I was about to kill this carp. I was frustrated at my bad luck and upset about bending the hook. My shoulders slumped as my knife hand fell to my side. I slowly slid the knife back in to its sheath and looked at the carp in sorrow. I figured it would probably die anyway.

Wait! Maybe I can save it, I thought. I snapped to attention and reached down for the fish. The carp gave little resistance as I gently slid my hands under it and placed it tenderly back into the water. I slowly rocked it back and forth in the life-giving liquid of the river. The fish soon responded by twisting and turning his body as he restored his strength.

It's working! I thought, as the rejuvenation of the carp was almost complete. Even the carp has a place in the river, I realized, as I let my hands go loose. The carp hesitated and stayed still for just a moment or so, then gave one big kick with his tail and shot out free into the open water.

5

ONE LAST CAST

For a moment, I just stood there. I watched as salmon jumped in the distance. I was bewildered. No salmon for me. My arms were sore. I had bent one of my good hooks. And it was getting late.

What a bunch of bad luck! I thought as I glanced backward and plopped my butt on the sand.

What am I doing here? What am I doing selling cars? What am I doing with my life? I questioned, as I pondered my luckless predicament. As I squinted at the setting sun, I realized I had an hour or so of sunlight left. And there I was without a flashlight.

Oh, well, I should be heading back anyway, I thought. I searched for a place to brace my hand to stand up. As I struggled to rise up, my waders squished and the safety belt hugged my chest, making breathing hard.

"Damn safety belt. I knew I didn't need you," I said out loud as I reached for the release buckle with both hands and prepared to set my chest free from its grip. I grabbed the right side and pinched the release. It wouldn't budge. I squeezed harder. The damn thing was stuck. "Oh, forget it!" I screamed as I gave up and searched for my gear.

I took one last look around and noticed the wind was picking up a bit and the sun was slipping away. The path to the car would be pitch dark if I waited too long.

I began a short debate in my mind. Should I go or make just one more cast? *Okay, Deyoung, name me one fisherman who doesn't make one more cast,* I easily justified to myself.

I glanced upward and noticed the marvelous golden hue of the late evening sky as the sun began its slow drop over the awaiting horizon. I stared in awe. I never tire of sunsets.

"No, gotta go," I argued again. But my body automatically started going through the routine of preparing to make that last cast. I set down my pole and slung off my creel. I remembered that one of the hooks was bent, so I reached into my pocket for the needle-nose pliers to bend the hook back as best I could.

I held the treble hook firmly against a large rock with my left hand and strained to twist it back straight with my right. I managed to get it to look like the other two hooks. "It'll have to do," I determined. I dropped the lure and let it hang free on the line. I again surveyed the river for a good spot.

The wind was blowing. I strained my eyes and I looked up at the beautiful sky, just standing there motionless, rod in hand. Realizing I had better cast, I figured the spot below the fall would do just fine. Flipping over the bail, I double-checked the lure length from the tip. A little long, but should be fine, I figured. I wheeled my arm back and, in one swift motion, released the lure toward the pending dusk.

I watched it fly toward the river. It arched high into the golden sky on what seemed like a perfect line to the pool. *Good spot,* I thought.

Suddenly, a large gust of wind blew in from the left side and seemed to grab the lure and push it toward the raging waterfall. "No!" I screamed, flipping the bail and desperately pulling the line back to avoid a snag.

"Dang wind!" I screamed. The lure began to fall, and I realized I had let out too much line. As if in slow motion, the lure plunged toward the raging waterfall.

"Oh, geez!" I shouted as I fought to keep the line and lure from being sucked into the jumble of rolling foam and rocks. No luck! As the lure plunged into the water, it was immediately captured and taken straight down into the dangerous currents that lay below the waterline.

As I scrambled down the sandbar, I worried I would lose the lure. I felt it turn and twist in the turbulence of the waterfall. Suddenly the line stopped dead and began to sag. I slowly started to reel in the line in the hopes of avoiding a snag.

Looking good so far, I thought with false confidence as I gingerly reeled the line in. The lure stopped dead in its tracks. "What? Darn it!" I cursed. I lifted the rod higher and tried to pull the lure in. The rod arched to a breaking point. I knew I was in trouble. I imagined the treble hooks sunk into an underwater log or stuck between some boulders.

"Shoot! Now, I really am going to lose this lure!" I tugged with futility on the line. I pulled hard on the pole, causing it to arch toward the water and strain the rod tip again.

I contemplated cutting the line, making a move for my knife. At that very moment, the line twitched and slowly began to move to the right. I wondered if it had broken free. The line slowly continued to move. I reeled in the sagging line. Suddenly the line went straight. I raised the rod to test for another snag.

"Wait a minute; wait just a minute." I felt a familiar sensation, a tugging on the other end of the line. I wondered if it could be a fish. My heart started to race. I carefully felt the line. It was still drifting toward me.

I decided to be proactive and meet up with it on the right bank. I raised the rod tip carefully and slowly walked down the sandbar.

Turning toward the water, I decided to wade out a little bit in case it was a fish. I did not want to spook it. Being careful to keep the line tight, I carefully waded out about three feet and planted myself firmly. Whatever it was, I could see it coming right at me now.

The line was getting shorter as I continued to reel. It was coming in too easy. It couldn't be a fish. The setting sun, slowly disappearing behind some sparse evening clouds, was making it hard to see. I looked for the best angle to peer into the darkening water to solve the mystery of whatever my lure was caught on.

I didn't have much time left. I had to see what was down there and quickly make my way back to the car before it got too dark. My eyes strained to see below the wavering waterline. As it got closer, the object began to slow considerably. I began to strain hard as I reeled in the line. *What the heck did I snag on? It's too heavy for a fish,* I estimated. It felt as if I was pulling in an old log. My arms began to ache.

The darkening skies made focusing hard as I struggled to make out whatever it was I snagged. I caught a brief glimpse of something large. It just had to be an old log.

Maybe I can drag it in and save the lure, I hoped. I gave the line a sharp tug. *Darn, it's heavy,* I thought, as the lined strained.

A sudden cold breeze made a shiver shoot down my spine.

Suddenly, the setting sun broke free from the evening clouds, its bright rays lighting the clear water. The water settled for a split second, and suddenly something became very clear!

"Good lord! It can't be. It just can't be!"

I stared in disbelief as the sun caught the object moving in the water. This time there was no mistake.

"It's a salmon! It's the mother of all salmon!" I yelled, as if I had an audience. It was the biggest salmon I had ever seen. It moved around like a small submarine. I stood there, stunned, not believing my eyes.

My mind raced a thousand miles an hour. I gauged the fish to be roughly five feet long, weighing ninety pounds or more, easily a new state or world record! *I have caught a world record salmon,* I thought triumphantly.

6

Who Caught Whom?

I quickly determined that I needed to set the hook on this big boy. Old reactions took over as I planted my feet and dropped the rod tip toward the huge salmon.

"Tighten the line now," I assured myself, "and wait until this guy turns away." Suddenly, the fish turned upstream and straightened the line taut.

"The time is now or never." I leaned forward and prepared my arms and body for the hard pull backward. "Now!" I exclaimed. My mind triggered my arms in an upward motion and I pulled the pole up with all my strength.

The bow of the rod told the tale as it bent sharply toward the water. "I got him. I got him!" I yelled out loud as I scrambled to position myself on the sandy bar. I held the rod tip high and, for just a split second, the line did not move, almost as if stuck on a concrete block. Then I gave a small tug and all hell broke loose.

The monster salmon, realizing it was hooked, took one shake and then headed downstream. Bracing to resist, I ground my feet into the gravel.

Zziiiinnggg! The line peeled off as fast as I had ever seen it go! "Whoooheee!" I screamed as I looked toward the setting sun and saw the huge salmon take off across the water. It was amazing.

It was surfacing at rhythmic intervals, right in the shimmering water, as it made its bid to escape. The screaming sound of my drag snapped me out of the momentary daze this amazing sight prompted.

Zziiinnnggg, zziiinng, my reel screamed as large intervals of monofilament shot from the reel at an astonishing pace. *Zziinngg Zzinnngg!* "Damn, at this rate I will be free-spooled in ten seconds," I warned myself. That would be the end of the line and a certain fish break-off for me, and I tried in vain to adjust the drag tighter. The line was as tight as I dared try without breaking it. Still the line screamed. I quickly made the decision to follow the fish as I scrambled to my left down the sandbar.

Straining to keep the rod tip held high, I realized that if the fish did not slow down I was soon going to run out of sandbar. As its end rushed toward me, the weight of the salmon pulled me toward the water.

"Man, oh man!" I exclaimed in awe. The salmon bent the rod toward the open water. I broke hard at the water's edge and searched for options. I quickly gauged the distance to the other side of the small inlet that the sandbar had formed. I thought I may have to wade across, but the decision was made for me. The force of the fish pulling on the line thrust me into the water.

I continued to fight the salmon as I splashed ungracefully into the cold water and made a dash for the safe footing of the far riverbank. I determined it was about sixty feet. I was hoping it was not too deep as I struggled with the salmon and the uneven river bottom. The fighting salmon led me deeper into the water.

"Oh no!" I yelled, realizing the water was at my waist and was quickly reaching my chest. I had misjudged the depth. Any deeper would be dangerous. I hesitated for a split second. Was it worth it to catch this monster? Heck yes, I concluded as I plunged forward. I knew this was easily a state record . . . and worth big money! I had to go for it. I gripped the rod as I held it above my head and surged toward the other side.

I could feel the river bottom rise gradually to the other side. The water receded down to my waist as I managed to reach other side's rocky shoreline. For a brief moment, I relished the safety of being there. But an abrupt hard jerk of my arms quickly snapped me to attention. Suddenly I had a new predicament: I was in the fight of my life with a monster salmon. As I struggled with the awesome fish, I glanced down the shoreline to assess the land.

The riverbank ran about a hundred yards until it dead-ended at a large tree root that thrust out from the riverbank. It was entangled throughout with weeds and branches, bordered by an impassable barrier of shrubs and bushes that continued down the bank and out of view. The water looked fairly shallow there. The setting sun reflected off the water's edge. It was getting dark, but that was not my biggest worry.

The huge salmon finally slowed. I followed the river's edge, being ever so careful to keep the rod high and the line tight. I did not want to give this baby a chance to break off. The power of this fish amazed me. I never took one hand off the rod and never had less than a complete grip pressure with my hands. I couldn't take the chance. This was a once in a lifetime salmon . . . and he was mine.

I stumbled, jumped, and hopped through the riverbank's morass of rock and shrub and driftwood, barely managing to keep an eye on the fish as I followed it down the river. As it slowed to a stop, I foolishly took the liberty of reeling in a small bit of fishing line. I braced the pole against my lower belly and let go with my left hand. I reached down quickly and grabbed the reel handle. One turn, two turns. I saw I had maybe fifty feet of line left.

Wham! The huge salmon felt the tug and took off. *Zzziiingg* went the last of the line as the salmon turned deep and, in one sharp motion, kicked his tail and flipped into the sky.

"Woooowww!" I shouted, as the huge salmon flew out of the water about a hundred feet in front of me. It soared up into the sky, leaving a trail of water that glistened in sunset colors. The silvery king seemed to freeze in midair about four feet out of the water, then twisted and turned his massive body in show of frustration for being caught. A flash of light caught my eye as I saw Grandpa Tak's lure holding strong in the salmon's mouth. I held the line firm and pulled hard, leaving no doubt in the salmon's mind that the fight was on!

Before the salmon descended back into the depths, it gave one last twist and turned right at me. For a split second, he seemed to look directly in my eyes.

I blinked, and when I opened my eyes he was gone, with nothing but a huge splash in his trail. *Wuuump!* The water surged high from the splash. My line dropped down deep and then turned again. Once more, the huge fish hurled himself out of the water. *Fwooosh . . . wuuump . . . fwooosh . . . wuuump* was the sound he made in a series of valiant leaps toward the setting sun in a desperate attempt to shake the hook.

I slipped and stumbled up and down the shoreline in a futile attempt to maintain control. But it was evident who had control: the salmon.

The fish was leading me all over, and my arms were beginning to ache. The adrenaline was wearing off, but I was determined to gain a second wind. As I pulled hard on the rod, the pole bent toward the large salmon. I reached down quickly and turned the reel handle as best I could under the power of the fighting fish. It felt like I was reeling in a huge log as I managed to take in about thirty yards of line. The fish seemed to tire from the leaps and slowed in the deep pool. I took the liberty of making a couple more turns of my reel, but the salmon took off again!

"Oooohhhh, shhoooot!" I yelled as he dragged me left again toward the root pile. The salmon must have decided he'd had enough of the jumping show and was headed for some underwater structure to dislodge the hook. "He's a smart one!"

Suddenly it was obvious: I had to put this pole to the full test. I tried to brace myself against being dragged totally downstream. I reeled furiously as I raced the fish down the shoreline, trying to cut him off before he got to the tangled mass of roots and branches.

I scaled a small rock and jumped out into the water, wading to about four feet, and there I tried to make my stand. I raised the rod tip high and with all my strength worked to turn the fish. The fish, feeling the new resistance, fought with full force and then suddenly turned back upstream.

"Yes!" I shouted in victory. The line grew less taut, allowing me to bring in more valuable line. I reeled hard and pumped the rod up and down in rhythm as I worked this giant toward the shore. For a brief moment, I thought about landing him.

Wrong! The salmon regained his strength and burst back upstream with the force of a powerboat. Once again the line screamed, as if in pain.

Zziiing, zing, zzzzinng! "Good lord!" I exclaimed. I lost all of the ground I had gained. More importantly, the line was peeling out again and it was time to run.

I took off back down the sandbar and retraced my path toward the inlet, following the salmon as he jetted back toward the waterfall. I couldn't let him get toward the falls. I realized I would have to cross the inlet again. Trying to slow down to a fast walk, I pulled hard on the pole, trying desperately to slow the fish so I could look for a spot where I could get out of the water. At least I would know how deep it was there, I figured, as I glanced about for the exit point.

I slowed to a brief stop near the water's edge and stared across to the other side. "Oh, geez. What the—?" is all I could manage to say. I stared in disbelief. Was it that far away to the other side? I quickly tried to assess the distance and what lay in between.

Well, it made no difference. With a big jerk, the fish pulled me into the water. I splashed into the inlet and stumbled for footing. I waded across the deep water. The salmon, sensing that I was in trouble, doubled his effort to pull free and charged hard again upstream.

Oh no! I thought, as the water crept above my waist. I was being dragged in and was stumbling. I kept going deeper until the water was close to my chest. Danger time! *I don't want to drown!* I scrambled for options. I focused on the sandbar ahead and estimated I had maybe thirty feet to go. I was struggling against the water as my feet gave way. I had stepped into a hole, and my whole body plunged below the waterline.

Dear God, Smolts . . . you're in frickin' big trouble, I screamed to myself as I bobbed on the river floor. My whole body was under water except my arms and hands. Seconds mattered. I held my breath as one arm, one hand, and my fishing rod—with the salmon still fighting—swung wildly above the water. My other hand waved around as if trying to paddle to the shore. How funny it must have looked, just a hand and fishing pole flailing about above the waterline. But no humor prevailed as utter panic entangled my whole being. I instinctively reached for my safety harness to make sure it was tight.

It was, thank God! I knew without a tight harness my waders would quickly fill with water and weigh me down, making escape impossible and death likely.

I froze as my eyes stared up through the clear water at the now-setting sun. How fabulously beautiful were the colors, and how insane was the moment. I had, for a second, entered some deadly altered state of consciousness.

I continued to move my feet as they slid and slipped on the

mossy rocks below. I had to get across, but I was making little progress.

My lungs screamed in desperation for air. My mouth opened slightly and took in a little water. *Keep your mouth closed, Deyoung!* my mind screamed, as I got a small taste of the river. My consciousness started to fade with the setting sun. I took one last look up. The lack of oxygen was draining my brain. My life flashed before me . . . my wife, my boys, . . . my family . . . my whole, seemingly hopeless life, one split second prompting a smile and the next utter fright. It wouldn't be long now, I prayed.

Suddenly the huge salmon took off with a burst. The force on the pole yanked my arm so hard that my body followed. My mind snapped to and I started churning my feet again on the rocks below, trying to regain solid footing. Suddenly the river bottom gradually started to rise up to the safety of the sandbar.

It was nothing short of amazing! The huge salmon seemed, in my stupor, to be pulling me out of the water as my face and head rushed upward and my upper body mercifully burst into the twilight sky.

I screamed as I burst out of the water and gulped the cool evening air, shaking my head like a wet dog as I gasped back to life and tried to stand erect. After regaining my composure, I opened my eyes to the lovely sight of stars set in a fabulous evening sky. I promised myself never to take that sight for granted again.

The night had overtaken the day. I continued to breathe deeply, filling my oxygen-starved lungs to capacity and sending energy to my weakened body. I burst up the bank, shaking from head to toe, and screamed with all my heart.

"Wooooohoooo! Yeah, baby!" I yelled as water streamed from my pockets and soaked clothing and left a wet trail up the sand as I scrambled to higher ground.

I shouted in delight and danced a short jig on the sandbar. I held the rod up and quickly realized the monster salmon was still attached to it.

"Yeah, baby—let's get it on!" I yelled as I went back into fighting mode with renewed vigor. I pulled hard up on the pole and set the drag on maximum. I reeled hard, stretching the thirty-pound test to the full limit. They will pay royalty money to me just to advertise the line, I thought, as it held up to way past its prescribed limit.

No fewer than four times, the fish made the run for the safety of the turbulence below the waterfall. And no fewer than four times, I fought to turn him back toward calmer water. The time stretched on. It had been easily forty-five minutes, maybe an hour, fighting this behemoth, and we both began to wear.

But I was making ground now. I turned the massive fish and slowly pulled him toward me. At that point I noticed my arms were starting to feel like gelatin again. The force of the fish took its toll. No time to quit now. I doubled my effort. The large fish seemed to be giving up. I towed it toward me. It gave just a token kick or two as I reeled harder and faster.

Finally making some headway with the fish, I glanced about for a place to land it. In the light of the rising moon, I saw a large rock with a smaller one below it—a likely spot. I walked in the water to greet the salmon.

From the tension of the line and arch of the pole I could tell the fish was maybe forty feet away from me now. Sensing victory, I waded out a little farther and pulled harder. At that moment, the moonlight shone through the water in front of me as I noticed a large log underwater.

"Oh! That's just great!" I said mockingly. I realized the salmon could get snagged in the log. It jutted out straight out into the river. Branches snag anything that drift by, and this one had snagged a bunch of debris.

I looked desperately for a different place to land the fish, but it was too late. The current took the salmon directly over to the log.

"Be careful, Smolts," I yelled as I lifted and twisted the rod in a futile attempt to avoid the tangling branches. The salmon took one small dive and cut under the log at the farthest point out. I tried gently to pull him back.

The fish briefly struggled and then flipped over the highest branch of the log. I strained to see if it was clear of the log. The fading sunset made for terrible underwater viewing. I gave the line one hard pull and was met with a taut line.

I screamed, "No! It can't be stuck!" I peered intently into the water. I could see the fish not ten feet away, yet it was stuck on a branch and not going anywhere. How could it be stuck? I knew the line was clear from the log. I looked again, my eyes straining. I could see the massive fish lying tranquil by the branch, almost nose to branch. Its massive body swayed in the current.

"Arghhh!" I yelled as the water surface became calm and I could see that one of the treble hooks was stuck on a branch and the other two were stuck in the fish. He looked like a blimp tied to a tall building as it swayed in the current. I pulled on the line to see how hard it was stuck on the branch, only making things worse.

"Damn, that hook will never come out." I knew once it set into a waterlogged log, it was in there for good.

I froze for a moment and my body limped in frustration. What was I going to do now? I couldn't swim out there. If I got stuck on the log, I could seriously hurt myself. I grabbed the rod firmly with both hands and pulled. Maybe the hook was weak. Then I flashed back to the carp.

Maybe, just maybe, the hook that was caught on the log was the weak hook, the one I had had to bend back in place when I released the carp. Maybe there was a chance!

I sprang back to life. I decided to put constant pressure on the hook to see if I could bend it free. The good hooks would not bend, but maybe I'd get lucky. I tugged with all my strength, pulling on the line so hard that I sensed that either the hook was going to bend or the line was going to break. I felt the monofilament stretch to the limit as the resistance was getting to be too much for the thirty-pound test line. *How can that line be holding?* I wondered. Slowly, I sensed the hook begin to bend toward me.

"It's bending!" I yelled. The hook slowly tweaked toward me. A little more was all I needed. I continued the constant pressure on the hook. It slowly bent.

Free! The massive salmon broke free and briefly caught the current.

The giant fish seemed to give up as I worked frantically to reel him in. I turned toward the shore, never taking my eyes off this marvelous creature as I pulled with all my strength. I got up on a small rock and pulled him ever closer.

"Oh my God . . . oh my God!" I yelled as I saw the salmon up close. He was beyond huge. I reached down and grabbed his enormous jaw and pulled him toward me with all my strength.

"Holy mother of all king salmon! This can't be real!" I yelled over and over. He was at least five feet long and maybe, just maybe, more than a hundred pounds!

I wondered how I was going to get this monster to the shore—and how was I going to get him home. He was too big to haul up on the rock, so I struggled around to the side where the sand and rock met. I could barely pull the salmon with my left hand. I held the pole with my right and stepped on a small, half-submerged rock to drag it up to the sandbar.

I turned toward the fish and pulled him into a shallow pool in the sand. The monster fish, to my surprise, put up no further resistance. "There. I got him! I got him!" I screamed as I rose up in jubilation.

Suddenly my scream went from joy to panic as my foot slipped on a slimy rock and I spun sideways, flailing my arms as my life flashed before me for the second time that day. I was falling toward the large rock to my side. I spun wildly in a desperate attempt to save my balance. The large rock rushed toward me as one hand still held a death grip on the rod and the other a death grip on the stringer. My elbows offered no cushion to the granite surface as it rushed toward my exposed shoulder and head.

Wham! My head hit the rock. This time I was out cold.

7

WHO'S THERE?

"Yuungth Thsmolz."

"Huh?" I said groggily.

"Heyy, Dyuunth Thmoltz!"

Coming to, I reflexively corrected whoever was trashing my name. "That's Deyoung Smolts!" I declared as I shook my head. "Who said that? Who's there?" I demanded, fully expecting one of the other fishermen had come to my rescue.

I rubbed the spot on my head where it had struck the rock. "Owww, that hurts," I said. I checked for blood. None. Relieved, but still bewildered, I lay there sprawled, half of me sitting in the water and the other half lying on the shore by the large rock. "Owwwww," I moaned. The initial shock went away, but my head was throbbing.

It was almost dark as I glanced around. The moon offered little help, and the trees shaded most of its light. "I'm okay," I responded to the faceless voice, "but what about my salmon?" I looked frantically to my side. "Yes! He's still there," I shouted in utter joy. In my stupor, I suddenly realized what I had just managed to do: catch what was very likely a state-record salmon.

But I dared not spook him while putting him on the stringer. He was still hooked. I unraveled the rope and grabbed the steel-tipped end. I reached in and quickly grabbed the huge salmon at his mouth and slid the steel shaft through his gill and up through his mouth. Done!

"Whaat the hellgg arrgh yub doinghh?" the same voice said as the fish fought the stringer.

"I've got you!" I screamed. But I suddenly realized that someone just said something to me. "Who said that? Who's out there?" I yelled, looking frantically around. I turned and stared into the pitch-black woods. "Who's there?" I angrily yelled again, trying to sound intimidating.

"No one there. Maybe just the wind," I thought to myself, or perhaps just the after-effects of being out cold.

"Gheeet thiis fwickkehn hwook oout of mwhee," the voice said again.

No wind that time. I had clearly heard a human voice. "That's it! Who's out there?" I yelled into the darkness.

"Geett thiiis hwookk out!"

"Whaaa?" I said as I fell back, realizing *the fish* was the voice. "What the heck? This can't be real!" I scrambled up to my knees and blinked my eyes at the writhing fish, wondering if I had hurt myself more seriously than I realized.

Suddenly the fish turned in the water and stared straight up at me. "Gweet thhes dammb hwoock outh of mmy mwwoofth!"

My head was still throbbing. *What the hell was he saying? Geth this damb hook oug of its mooth . . . geth dis dam hook outh ob moouf . . . oh my gosh, the salmon was saying, "Get this damn hook out of my mouth!"*

My jaw dropped and my body stiffened. I repeated it all again in my woozy head: "Get this damn hook out? Get the hook out . . . get the hook out!" My eyes shifted from the salmon's eyes to where the two hooks were deeply embedded in his huge jutting jaw.

"Oh my gosh. Those must hurt," I said as I reached for my needle-nose pliers. I flipped them open and bent down to the fish.

A salmon just talked to me, I kept repeating in my head. *But it couldn't have,* I thought. I opened his jaw and reached in.

"Bweehh carghbull . . . ," the salmon said.

"Ahh!" I yelled as I jumped back again. *Be careful? Did he just say "be careful"? I know he said something that time.* "What the hell am I doing? Where am I?" I stammered, my head swimming.

Slowly and carefully, I removed the large, sharp treble hooks. Not in too deep, I noticed. The hooks slid out easily, as if the fish knew to be still. Confused and not knowing what to expect next, I actually listened to myself calmly ask the fish, "Now. Is that better?"

"Yes, that's better," The salmon said, very clearly this time.

"Whoa!" I yelled as I jumped back a little. "What? You *can* talk!" I shouted.

"Yes. I can talk, and you don't need to yell. I can hear, too."

"Well, how come I can understand you better now?" I asked hesitantly.

"Hey, you would sound garbled, too, if you had a couple hooks and a spinner stuck in your face. Wouldn't you, young Smolts?"

"It's Deyoung Smolts," I snapped back. I reached to put the pliers away. "And how do you know my name anyway?"

"Don't put those away yet!" the huge salmon responded. "I need a favor."

"A favor? What?" I asked with suspicion.

"Look at the other side of my jaw," the fish said somberly.

"The other side of your jaw? What's wrong?" I inquired as I peered around the football-sized head of the fish. I spotted a large, old-style hook stuck deep into the salmon's other side. "Oh, I see."

"Can you take that hook out, too?" he asked.

"Sure, no problem," I said, not thinking about how insanely crazy this was. After all, when you find yourself conversing with a fish, it is apparent the day has taken a dramatic turn. There I was, sitting in the dark, talking with a fish as if it was my dog.

And the fish understood me better. *How injured am I?* I wondered. I reached down with the pliers and used the wire cutter to cut the eye off the hook, then I gripped it and gently slid it out clean.

"Wow! Amazing," I said. "That is an old hook. What is the story on that one? How long have you had it stuck in you?" I asked, babbling my sentences together.

"Oh, it's a long story. A long time ago," the great fish answered almost sadly. Then he snapped to and said loudly, "Now it's time to let me go, young Smolts."

"Oh, no," I answered quickly. "Hey! How is it you know my name?" I asked the fish.

"I can't really tell you—" the fish started to say before I cut him off.

"What's your name?" I blurted out. "You have a name?"

"My name? My name is Salvador, but my friends call me Sal. Now, are you going release me?"

"Well, I'm afraid I can't do that, Sal," I said cagily.

"Hey! It's Salvador," he quickly corrected. "I said my *friends* call me Sal."

"Oh . . . ," I said, somewhat stunned. "Okay, Salvador, I can't let you go. Let me explain. You are worth a lot of money to me. I can sell the rights to the lure I used to catch you and the rod and all the gear. I will be famous and on television. My wife and kids will be proud of me. I just can't let you go. I can't do it. Sorry . . ." my voice trailed off as I came to the realization that I would have to kill this magnificent creature to score my imagined rewards.

"Why do you need the money?" Salvador shot back.

Man, he has some attitude, I thought to myself, stymied for a good answer.

"You would have a bad attitude, too, if you thought you were going to die," Salvador said smartly.

"What the—? You can read my thoughts, too?" I asked, staring at Salvador.

"I can do many things," Salvador answered. "So, tell me why you need the money, young Smolts."

"It's Deyoung Smolts!" I shot back, perturbed at his missing the *De* in Deyoung.

"Yeah, whatever," Salvador replied flippantly. "Why do you need the money?" he said, hammering at me again.

"I need it to pay bills and stuff . . . and buy a new car," I said defensively. "And my house needs some work, and the boys . . ."

"I see," said Salvador. "How come you can't pay your bills?"

"Because sales are slow at work and I'm running out of money in my savings," I stated matter-of-factly. "And I can't—"

Salvador interrupted. "I get it. I get it. You can't sell any cars, and therefore you don't have the money—is that right?"

"Yes! That is the root of all my problems," I responded, realizing with a start that the fish knew what I did for a living in addition to my name.

Now angered, I looked around for something to club the smart-aleck salmon with.

"Hey, wait a minute, young fella!" Salvador said as he saw me glancing around. "You're not going to club me, are you?" he asked. He kicked his tail wildly in a futile attempt to get free of the stringer.

"Okay, be careful! Calm down, calm down," I said. Water splashed all over. I double-checked the rope. This fish could read my mind. I had to be careful what I said—I mean, thought.

Salvador calmed down, but then he snapped right back with another zinger: "How come you can't sell any cars?"

"I don't know. I'm just unlucky, I guess," I replied.

"Yeah, unlucky," Salvador said. "How about when you blew off that lady this morning, and she turned around and bought a car from Rick Painter?"

"What? How do you know about that?" I shot back. "Besides,

she told me she was looking for the parts department," I added sheepishly.

Salvador then asked, almost in disgust, "Did you ask her when she was done with parts whether she wanted to look at cars? Did you even give her a chance to talk—to become a prospect?"

"Uh, no, I guess I didn't," I said, my voice trailing off as I responded.

Salvador, feeling he was on a roll now, dug in deeper. "How many appointments did you have last month? How many ups did you have? How many demo drives? How much did you average per deal? What sales training books are you reading? Are you practicing daily? Do you have a monthly planning guide?"

"I don't know ... no ... none ... I don't know ... no," I answered.

"You have no direction. No goals, young Smolts, and you need *my* help," Salvador asserted.

"Your help? *Your help?* I don't need your help. I just need you to be still and quiet so I can figure out what to do with you. And it's *Deyoung*!" I said emphatically.

"Yes, young Smolts, you need my help," Salvador said. "So I'll tell you what I am going to do. I am going to make you a deal."

"Make *me* a deal?" I said, shocked at this fish's gall. "How are you going to make *me* a deal? I am the one who has you on the rope, and I am the one who is going to take you to the local bait shop to weigh and measure you. And you have nothing I want anyway," I said.

"I am going to make you a trade," said Salvador.

"A trade? For what? What do you have, a belly full of gold nuggets?" I joked.

"Oh, I have something you need, Smolts. I have something you need . . . ," Sal said, his voice becoming softer to gain my attention.

I took the bait, seeing how serious this fish was. "Okay, Salvador. What do you have that is worth more than I am going to make off you?"

"Knowledge," Salvador said tersely.

The truth was, in the back of my mind I really didn't want to kill this beautiful fish anyway. So I pressed on. "Knowledge . . . about what? What kind of knowledge can *you* give *me*?" I asked suspiciously.

"Knowledge about sales . . . *and about life*. Knowledge you need to make a living," Salvador said. "Knowledge that would normally take you years—if not a lifetime—to learn."

I was very interested now because I knew I was doing terribly at work and was on the verge of getting fired. I straightened up a little and said, "Okay, tell me more."

Sal continued. "I will give you knowledge on how to sell more cars, how to make more appointments and profit, how to have a better customer satisfaction rating, and generally how to be more successful in life. I will also teach you character and strength of heart, philosophies and ideals you will need in your life. And, with this knowledge, I promise you will make more money in your lifetime than you can ever make off of me."

He had my full attention now. So I asked, "How do I know you will really help me?"

"I guarantee I will help you. In the end, if I have not helped you to your satisfaction, then you can kill me," he stated confidently with a resolve easy to admire.

"Kill you? You make it sound so barbaric. You know, Salvador, I actually don't want to kill you," I said almost apologetically.

"Then it's a deal?" Salvador asked intently.

"What a minute," I said. "How are you going to help me? We are stuck out on the river, and it's almost pitch black out. How are you going to give me the knowledge I need out here in the middle of nowhere?"

"You leave that part up to me, young Smolts," Salvador replied with confidence. Of course, he could read my mind and knew I was about to take him up on his offer. "So, do we have a deal?

"Yessss, we have a deal," I said. "Do we need to shake on it or something?" I asked, trying in vain to lighten the moment.

"No, your word will do. Just as you have my word that, when I am done, if you are happy with your newfound knowledge, then you will set me free, and, as I said, if you are not satisfied, then you can kill—"

"Okay, okay, just don't say *kill* again," I shot back. "You have my word. So now what?"

"Great!" Salvador shouted. "We better get this fish in the water. Time's a-wasting. Now, young Smolts, I want you to close your eyes and hold your breath."

"Huh?" I asked in confusion. "Close my eyes? How do I know I can trust you?"

"You know you can," Salvador said reassuringly. "Okay, Deyoung, compose yourself. This has been the weirdest day of your life, so you might as well go with the flow and just do what I say, okay? Now, close your eyes and take a deep breath."

Here goes, I thought as I shut my eyes. I then exhaled and drew in a deep breath.

Salvador, seeing I was ready, shouted, "Here we go!"

At that moment, I felt a little dizzy. I could feel my body straighten up as I dove into the cold river and started kicking with what I thought were my legs and feet. I was completely submerged. My ears felt instant pressure and filled with the sound of the churning, gurgling water.

What the heck? I wondered, as my body stayed easily below the water. I opened my eyes and glanced to my side and could see a large salmon swimming next to me. "Salvador? Salvador? Is that you?" I asked.

"Yes. It's me," Salvador said, noticing I still had my mouth tightly closed. "You can stop holding your breath now. You can now breathe underwater . . . and see and hear and do everything that I or any other salmon can do," he assured me.

"And from now on," he added as he swam alongside me, "you can call me Sal."

8

Fish Eye View

Hey, this is just fabulous! I thought for a moment as my ears and eyes adjusted to my surroundings. I gazed in amazement at my fisheye view from underneath the water, until I fully realized what this talking salmon had done.

"You turned me into a salmon?" I yelled.

"Whoa there, young buck!" Sal answered back. "You don't have to yell so loud. Yes, I turned you into a salmon."

"You turned me into a dang salmon?" I asked again. "I can't believe you turned me into a fish. A fish!" I continued to scream, for I was now hysterical and swimming madly in circles with *my new fish body*. "You turned me into a fish . . . ," I repeated, my voice trailing off.

"Hold on now, young Smolts, how else did you expect me to teach you? Huh? You didn't expect *me* to turn into a human, now did you? Really, did you?"

"Well, I don't know," I answered. "I didn't know what to expect. You could have warned me or something. You could have at least warned me," I repeated, slowly calming down and starting to regain a normal heartbeat.

I tried my best to look at myself. From what I could see with eyes on the sides of my fish head, I looked like a strong, young king salmon. I wasn't nearly as big as Sal, but I was healthy and fit with a magnificent, bright silver body. I figured I was about fifteen pounds of solid muscle. I flexed my pectoral fins. "Well, how do I swim? What do I do? Where are we going?" I asked.

"Just do as your body tells you," said Sal swimming along beside. "And as far as where we go, leave that up to me. Now, we have to see what kind of help you really need."

"What?" I asked. "What do you mean?"

"I am going to give you your first lesson, and that lesson is to fully evaluate a situation from various points of view and then determine the right way to make it better," Sal announced.

"But, hey, I thought you knew everything about me," I said with a smart-aleck tone.

"Oh, I see. Okay, you have a lot to learn," Sal replied in a somewhat-disparaging tone. "I know plenty about you, young Smolts. I just want to know what *you* think you need to learn," replied Sal.

As I thought of the things I wanted to learn, I noticed that my body was starting to get used to the surroundings. This will be great, I thought, as we circled in the large pool below the waterfall. The falls were just as I always assumed they would be, water boiling among tangled logs and large boulders. It looked scary.

"Okay, snap out of it, wonder boy," interrupted Sal. "Now, tell me what you want to learn."

"I want to be top salesperson. I want to sell the cars that have the most profit in them, no minimum commission advertised specials with no profit in them for me. I don't want to stand out on the point waiting for ups all the time. I want to be a manager someday . . . or even a general sales manager!" I proudly told Sal. My wants rolled off my tongue. I finished with, "And I want to take my family to Hawaii. Oh, and also I want one of those new Hummer SUVs that just came out."

"Whew! That's quite a list there, young Smolts, but—"

"Hey, that's *Deyoung* Smolts!" I boldly shot back.

"Okay, Smolts. I see you need more than I thought. I will have to start your lesson further back than I wanted."

"What?" I stuttered back. "What do you mean, Sal?"

"I will show you," said Sal. "I want you to picture something, okay, Smolts?"

Knowing at this point I had to do what he wanted from here on, I answered, "No problem, Sal."

"Okay, now picture this large river as your life," Sal said. "The mouth of the river is where you enter into adulthood, kind of like when you get out of high school. Do you follow me?"

"I think I am seeing it," I replied. I was beginning to see some parallels between a person's life and a river. "In life, we are, like, swimming upriver, right?"

"Yes! Good," Sal replied with an appreciative grin. "It is like we are swimming upstream. We enter the river of life at the stage when humans become adults, say eighteen or nineteen of your years."

"I see it now," I proudly replied. "The river represents your life from almost the beginning to its end."

"Yes! Yes, yes," replied Sal. "You've got it!" He nodded toward the waterfall ahead. "Picture those falls as the point in your life where you are now."

"The point I am right now?" I questioned, but I knew the answer already.

"Yes. You know what I mean, Smolts. We are about twenty-five miles upstream, with about another sixty or seventy to go. *Do you understand*?" he asked.

Well, I was no brain surgeon, but considering that I had just turned twenty-five, I figured I had this one figured out. "I'm with you, Sal," I answered.

"All right, so let's go!" Sal answered. And with unbelievable agility, he swung his massive frame toward the roaring waterfall.

"Hey! Where are you going?" I yelled. I tried to follow.

Sal answered, "It's not where am I going. It's where are *we* going."

As we slowed in a base area below the churning water, I started to notice flashes of darkness swim past at blinding speed as we disappeared deeper into the bubbly mass.

"What was that?" I asked Sal.

"Oh, those are our brothers on their way upstream."

"Wow, they are going fast," I answered.

"They are doing what it takes," Sal answered back.

"Now, Smolts, it's our turn."

"Our turn?" I said slowly and with a worried hesitation.

"Now, we will let our bodies float backward about fifty feet or so and then make a run up the falls. When we get up to the top, we will stop and meet up there," Sal said matter-of-factly.

"Well, that sounds good," I answered with a slight hesitation. "But why don't we just turn around and swim downstream?" I asked.

"What?" Sal asked pointedly.

"Yeah. You said we had to float backward and go back about fifty yards. Why?"

"Good question, young Smolts," Sal said. "I will now give you one of the most important lessons you can learn. Are you ready?"

"Uh, I think so," I answered.

"Always keep your nose pointed upstream," Sal said with a sudden firmness in his voice. "Let me explain. We are now facing upstream, right? And where are you looking?"

"I am looking in front of me and to the sides, Sal."

"Can you see behind you?"

I strained hard to look back, and I could see back just a little, but that was it. "Just a little," I answered as my eyes rolled back to the front.

As I said that, a large insect came floating by and—in an instant—Sal moved up and grabbed it before it could float away.

"I see, Sal," I said. "We look upstream because our food comes down that way." As I said that, something caught my eye and my body almost automatically moved as a large stick gushed by me in the oncoming current. "Whoa, that almost got me!" I screamed.

"That's right," said Sal. "Almost all things come from ahead—good or bad—so you must always be paying attention."

I sensed the lesson here, and I knew now it was okay to ask whatever questions I wanted. In a much calmer voice, I asked, "So keeping your nose upstream keeps you fed and keeps you safe from danger?"

"No. Keeping your nose upstream makes you *safer* from danger. But there are no guarantees, as my torn-up jaw shows you, eh, Smolts?" Sal said with a wink. "Also, when you look into the river and see fish, how many are pointed downstream?"

Good point, I thought. Yes, every fish I have ever seen swimming in a river is pointed upstream. As I glanced at the hook tears and marks on Sal's huge body, I knew what he meant. "No guarantees. And it's always a good idea to keep your nose pointed upstream. That's where the food comes from," I recalled with a smile as I now became increasingly hungry. Then I thought to ask, "Is that the key to my success?"

"The key?" he asked, wondering what I meant.

"Well, I'm asking if that is what I need to know to help me out in life," I said.

"Oh," Sal replied, finally seeming to understand what I was asking. "No, Smolts. Let me tell you something very important."

"What is that, Sal?"

"Do you know what a key master is?" Sal asked.

"Yeah," I replied. "He's the guy in medieval days who carried the keys to all the doors with him."

"Yes, that is correct. And you have to become like a key master. You will be given many, many keys—or lessons—on this journey, and when we are done here, it is up to you to use those keys to open the doors that you will need to pass through in life."

"I see," I answered. "So you're saying the goal is to have many keys at your disposal. That way you can open a multitude of doors if you have to. Right?"

"Yes! But also, don't assume that the first key, the second, or even the third key you try will always work. Don't make assumptions," Sal added. "Ask questions . . . communicate with others . . . have a clear vision of your path and goals to avoid misunderstandings and needless suffering. *Do you understand*?" he grunted.

"Okay, have many keys . . . don't assume *anything*. I'm learning a lot already, huh, Sal?"

"Yes. Yes. Good job, Smolts!"

"Okay then, *are you ready*?" I asked Sal as we kept our noses pointed upstream and drifted back about fifty yards.

The oncoming current in my face grew weaker as we drifted back. I had no idea what lay ahead. We set into a holding pattern just below the falls with about five or six other salmon. Every once in a while one would burst out of the group and hurdle into the raging foam. I was starting to get a little worried at this point because the noise of the falls seemed to grow as the time for our turn grew near.

Our turn was almost upon us. "Now, Smolts, when I go, you follow me and I'll meet you at the top of the falls," Sal said. "Try to minimize motion so you are moving at just enough speed for maximum effect," he yelled above the rushing sounds of churning water.

"Okay!" I answered, figuring that Sal knew what he was doing. With one swift kick of his massive tail, Sal took off like a rocket up the rushing waterfall. Up and up he swam magnificently until he reached the top, about twenty feet above the bubbling pool.

Seeing Sal go, I kicked my tail into gear and headed up the river. "Whoo hoooo!" I yelled. The foaming water enveloped my body as I flung myself up the roaring waterfall. "Whooaaa whhoo hoooo! This is fantastic!" I screamed. The rush of water flew by me and I sailed four to five feet up the falls. Suddenly, I began to slow down. *Better kick harder,* I figured. But kicking harder did no good, as the water's force against me seemed to grow.

"What the—" The force of the water hurtled me backward toward the raging pool that lay below.

"Whoooaaaaaa," I screamed. The tumbling water dropped me like a log into the tumbling mass of foam and bubbles. I felt like a rag doll for what seemed like forever, and just when I thought I was going to pass out, a sudden surge spit me out and I spun and tumbled furiously until I came to a slow drift, almost back at the spot where we had first started.

I floated there for a second, stunned, then I snapped out of it. I settled into a holding pattern facing upstream. "What the heck was that?" I screamed, looking around for Sal.

Sal was nowhere around. "Sal!" I yelled. "That damned fish! He left me here all alone . . . what am I going to do? Okay, I am going to try again," I told myself in confidence. I got in line for another try.

But then I heard voices yelling, "You won't make it . . . you won't make it!"

"Sal?" I asked out loud. I turned to look, but it wasn't Sal. It was a huddle of other salmon that were swimming by the side of the falls.

"You won't make it! You won't make it! It's too hard!" they shouted.

"What?" I yelled back. I stayed in line so as not to lose my place.

"The current is too strong from the rain, and there is too much debris in the water," the salmon shouted.

"Yeah! You won't make it!" another added.

"Come over here with us. Wait for a better time. We may just stay here, it's so nice."

For a brief moment, I thought maybe I should rest. But I had to make it up there and meet Sal. "I'll show them," I said to myself as I built up for another run. I geared up this time and used everything I had to burst up the raging falls.

"I'm going to make it up there!" I said as I butted heads with the rushing force of the water. I was doing well until about eight feet up, when my first burst of energy began to wane.

I could hear the salmon yelling from the swarm, "You can't make it. You can't make it!"

Then I thought, "Hey, maybe I *can't* make it." And then, like the first time, I slowed, stopped, and then tumbled backward to the turbulence below.

I tumbled furiously into the foaming abyss, smashing into the bottom reaches of the falls, my body hitting a branch that was wedged deep into the rock below the waterfall.

"Oww!" I screamed in pain. One of my bottom fins tore on a sharp stick, and then I struck the rock that it was wedged into. "Owww!" *What the heck is happening?* I wondered as I realized that I was completely stunned and could not move a fin or a gill! I started to freak out. The wild water tumbled me around and a current caught me and spit me back downstream for the second time that day.

But something was different this time; I was slowly floating up to the surface. I did not know what do, for I could do nothing in my paralyzed state. I broke the water's surface and began to float. I looked at the stars with one eye and floated down the river.

I slowly drifted downstream and remembered seeing the outlines of the towering oak trees with their limbs reaching out into the evening dusk, casting frightening shadows against the twilight-lit riverbank.

"What's that?" I asked myself. I saw a large object flash across the moon. "Hey, a bald eagle!" I saw it fly off and then make a long sweeping turn back toward the river across the full moon. As the eagle grew closer, it seemed to be picking up speed and heading right for me. Then I realized I was not Deyoung Smolts, the human. I was Deyoung Smolts, *the fish*! This eagle was headed right at me . . . and I could do nothing.

Instant panic shot through my body as I struggled to break free of my paralyzed state. I then noticed a little blood seeping out of my wound. I had been leaving a trail of blood in the water.

"Oh, geez, I'm in trouble!" Suddenly I heard a loud *screeeeeach*! I sensed that my end was near. I shut my eyes for a split second and then opened them. All I could see were two outstretched claws and the whites of the eagle's eyes as it descended upon me.

Kaaawhooom! The water, like a volcanic force, erupted below me and sent my body hurtling up into the late evening sky. Arching waves of glistening water rose with me as I tumbled through the cold night air . . . just in time to see Sal!

Sal hurtled up out of the water like a missile. He launched into the sky to meet the bald eagle head on, crashing into the shocked bird's side. The massive impact of a hundred pounds of pure muscle sent the eagle fluttering back up into the sky. With empty claws and the loss of a few feathers, the huge bird let out another load screech, then it quickly recovered and turned to fly back into the fading sunset.

Kuuuwuump, went the water as Sal came crashing down. He tumbled for a second and then gracefully righted himself to resume swimming upstream.

Hitting the safety of the water snapped me out of my paralyzed state, and I began to swim again. What a relief! I felt instant joy as I swam around—until I realized I was not swimming as well as I had before.

"Owwww!" I yelled again in pain from my damaged fin. And

a quick glance revealed it looked bad. I wondered what I would do next. I swam unsteadily back to Sal's side.

"Sal! Sal! You saved me!" I screamed in joy as I winced in pain. "But I'm hurt! I can't swim well . . . and the waterfall . . . and that eagle," I rambled. "I guess I am lucky to have a friend around like you to save me," I assured him.

"Yes, I saved you, young Smolts. I saved you," Sal said in a calm voice. "I would have done it for anyone, friend or not. But, young Smolts, how was your lesson?"

The bleeding had finally stopped on my fin, but my injury made it difficult to keep up with Sal.

"Lesson? Lesson? What lesson?" I answered, almost yelling. "You told me to follow you up the falls, and I tried. Then I came crashing down and got thrown around all over the place. And then these other salmon told the truth—the water was running too fast, making it impossible to swim up the falls!"

"But I tried again," I added, "and I got thrown back down the falls again . . . and became paralyzed, and had a bald fricking eagle almost eat me for dinner! Sure, I'm happy you saved me, but—"

"And what did you learn?" Sal simply asked.

"What did I learn? What did I . . . ," I yelled in frustration at Sal. "I learned I can't trust you! And I can't make it up that waterfall. And I learned what it's like to look a hungry bald eagle in its eyes. I learned that fish can feel pain, because my fin hurts! That's what I learned, Sal. Now is that what I came down here for? Is it? Is it?" I demanded.

"Well. Uh, okay, sorry about the eagle thing. That was a tad close, I admit," Sal said rather coolly. "Now, why do you think you did not make it up the waterfall?"

"What? Oh no," I answered. "I am done with this. I am not going to play this game. And if you think—"

"Smolts!" Sal uttered in a deep, penetrating voice, like a Samurai warrior talking to his troops. It snapped me into full and instant attention.

"Yes, Sal," I answered in a much more respectful tone.

"We are in *my* world now," Sal said in that voice again. "I am here to teach you what you need to know. So from here forward, do not give me anything but the most honest and sincere answer that you feel best fits the question. *Is that understood*?"

Well, I am no rocket scientist, but he did weigh a hundred pounds, and he had just saved me again, and I had agreed to let him teach me for some insane reason. So I knew from here on in, I was his student.

"Okay, Smolts. What did you learn?" Sal asked, then added, "Don't think . . . *feeeel*."

Don't think, feel . . . don't think, feel. I closed my eyes and recalled the water's force against my body as I entered the rapids and how it grew as I jumped higher into them. The rapids pushed hard against me. I just could not go farther, and I remembered the other salmon couldn't make it either.

"That's it!" I answered proudly after much thought. "I couldn't make it because the water was too fast from the recent storm. Even some of the other salmon couldn't do it."

"Oh, I get it," Sal responded. "The water was too strong, the other fish could not make it, and that is why you failed."

"Yes. That's it!" I asserted.

"I see we have a lot to learn. A lot to learn," Sal affirmed. Then he added something that hit me like a rock. "You see, you have to learn to fail before you can succeed. We have to go back to school."

"What?" I asked. "Why do I have to go back to school?"

"Because. Look over there, young Smolts," he said as he nudged me upstream.

I looked ahead and saw some salmon, all of them about the

same size and weight as me, swimming steadily in the current. Then, with a sudden burst, they all shot straight up into the falls and glided effortlessly up the next level. And then another, and another.

"What do you see?" asked Sal.

"Well, I see a bunch of salmon that look like me making it up to the next level. So what?"

"That is why we have to go back to school," Sal said. "You have a lot to learn, Smolts, a lot to learn. You see, there is no difference between you and those other salmon, but they made it up the falls with ease. And the reason? They had a path picked out in the falls, one that allowed them to make it up more easily. And they had practiced jumping up similar falls, so they knew what to expect. So in their minds, they *knew* they would make it up. They were not *trying* to make it. They were ready, not just physically, but mentally and emotionally. They were on a path," he asserted.

"But you, on the other hand, you are not ready—*you had no path,*" Sal admonished. "And always remember, if your path leads nowhere, you will surely get there. Just like you were not ready to become a top salesperson or a manager. So we have to go back to school, and you have to relearn what you do not know."

"Relearn? How will I do that?" I asked Sal. "And what school? Why can't you just tell me about your experience, and I'll learn from that?"

"Well, young Smolts, that's why I allowed you to fail going up that waterfall," he said in a tone that startled me. "The one thing about getting experience is you have to experience it to get it. Smolts, I can't just tell you all you need to know. I have to *show* you, because some things have to be seen before they can be believed. But before we go, I will need you to do something for me," Sal said with a concerned voice.

"Yes, Sal, anything you want," I said. I could see how serious and frustrated he was about my learning curve.

"You must empty your cup before you can drink my tea," Sal said.

"Empty my cup? What cup?" I asked, confused.

"Your mind. Your mind is like a cup, capable of being filled with knowledge. Your mind is now half-filled with the rancid knowledge that is poisoning the little good knowledge you do possess. I want you to empty your cup so I can fill your head with new knowledge that will help you on your journey."

"Why do I need to do that? Why can't I just, well, mix it with my knowledge?" I asked, still not getting it.

"You see," Sal continued, "with a half-full cup of tea, if I tried to fill it with an amount equal to a full cup, it would overflow and soak the holder in scalding hot tea. Do you see my point, young Smolts?"

"I see," I told Sal. "I will empty my cup—so I can drink your tea."

"Good!" Sal said. "And now it's time to go back to school."

"What is with this *back to school* thing? And what about my injury? I'm disabled."

"That little thing?" Sal said, almost laughing as he looked at my torn fin. "Smolts, are you dead?"

"No! I'm obviously not dead," I shot back.

"Then you are not disabled! Now, just close your eyes," Sal demanded.

"Can I ask you something first?" I asked in a hesitant tone.

"What is that?" Sal responded impatiently.

"Are you my master?" I responded tentatively.

"Your master?" Sal replied.

"Yeah. The master who will always be with me as I go through life?" I replied.

Sal smiled and said, "No, Smolts, I am not your master. But you will meet your master on this journey." His voice trailed off. "Now close your eyes."

Ohhh, no. Not that again, I thought, recalling the last time I had closed my eyes for him during that first dive into the water that had turned me into a salmon.

I slowly closed my eyes and trusted Sal to take me to his school. Whatever it was—and wherever it was.

9

Back to School

The sensations I felt after closing my eyes were quite different this time. For one thing, there was no dive into the cold water. The best way to describe it was that it felt like I was traveling through time . . . backward. All I felt was a constant, whooshing motion, and it felt really odd.

"You there, Smolts?"

"We can talk while we are in this state?" I asked.

"Yes, we can," Sal answered. "Do you feel okay?"

"Yes, I'm okay." Then I asked, "Are we going back in time?"

"Sort of. We are going back to the ocean, the place where your young life started. We are traveling back down the river, past the delta, and back into the Pacific Ocean—to meet my brothers."

"Wow! That sounds cool!" I replied in astonishment. "But I thought salmon were born in the river."

"They are, young Smolts. But we don't want to go that far back. We just want to go back to your youth and your teens. We will then continue your teaching."

"Oh, I see," I answered. "How much longer until we are there?"

Sal didn't answer.

With that, we began to slow down and, to my astonishment, we came to a grinding stop. "Ooow, spuut! The water is salty here," I sputtered to Sal as I tried to adjust my eyes.

"Hah, hah," Sal laughed. "Usually it takes some transition time to do what we are doing, going from fresh to salt water. We would have to slowly dive deep and let our gills and kidneys adjust so they can process the salt. But today we're making an exception," he said nonchalantly.

As my eyes regained focus, I could see nothing but clear blue water far into the ocean depths. "Wow. It's empty," I told Sal. I then felt a massive presence at my back. There behind me was the largest school of salmon I had ever seen. The infinite school stretched out from left to right as far as my fish eyes could see. It seemed to move as one in great sheets of silver and ribbons of gray reflecting sunlight. I had never seen such a sight.

"There must be a million salmon here!" I yelled as the huge school continued to pass by with flashing brilliance.

"More than a million, young Smolts. Well over a million," he said confidently.

"So, Sal, is this is what you meant when you said I have to go back to school: a school of fish?"

"Yes, Deyoung, we are back in school," answered Sal. "So, what do you see?" he asked as we watched the massive school continue to swim past.

Well, I knew better than not to answer, so I told Sal, "I see a bunch of salmon, and they look like they are all swimming in unison."

"Good. Good, Smolts. Now, what do you notice about these salmon?"

"I don't know," I replied. Then it dawned on me: they all looked the same. I saw nothing but silvery streaks in the endless wave of salmon that swam by. "That's it! They all look the same."

"Good. Now I am going to slow them down a little," Sal said. Then he let out a high-pitched sound, and the great wave of salmon began to slow, as if by magic.

"Now look," Sal pointed.

"What?" I asked as I looked hard at the salmon. I looked harder and I could see that the salmon were, in fact, all a little different. Some had dark markings, some light; some were small, others large; some were red, others silver. It was an odd mix of differences and similarities.

"They are all slightly different—and yet they are all the same," I told Sal. "But how can you and all these salmon be brothers?" I asked.

"Because we are the same, yet only slightly different. It's kind of like you humans.

We're all brothers under the skin. Do you get the lesson here, Smolts?" Sal asked emphatically.

"Yes, Sal, everyone is a brother, right?" I answered cautiously.

"Well, you're almost right," Sal offered with a smile. "A more appropriate metaphor is that every living creature has brothers, mothers, fathers, and sisters. Try to respect them all for who and what they are. After all, they are fighting the same fight we are."

"What fight is that?" I asked Sal.

"What fight? What fight, you ask?" Sal repeated as he turned for a split second to make eye contact with me. "Survival," he said, as his eyes locked on mine.

We stared into each other's soul for the split second I needed to fully understand the implications of this word. Just as suddenly, Sal turned his head away, flicked his tail, and burst ahead of me. And with a flick of mine, I shot forward to swim beside him again.

"Now we are ready to join the school," Sal yelled. And on that note, Sal burst toward the teeming mass as I tried to keep up. At first, we swam along the side of the awesome school. Then on cue, Sal nudged me and we swam our way into the group and became one with the others.

"What are we doing . . . and why do we do this?" I yelled to Sal as our bodies instinctively turned and twisted with the moving mass.

"We look for food, but we too are food," he warned. "There is no hiding for the hunted, so we must come together as one.

"We do this to save as many of our species as we can. Collectives come together to save the individual, much like your country and other countries do," Sal observed. "Now, work as a team. Become one with the team. Do as the school does. Look for the head salmon, and he will show you the way."

"Is he the master?" I asked.

"No. He is not the master. You will meet your master in good time," Sal assured me. "But it's important now to follow the school for a while. It will help you get in shape, not just physically but mentally as well."

"What do I do? How do I act?" I asked Sal.

"Just have fun," Sal answered teasingly.

"Have fun?" I answered, confused.

"Yes. Have fun. *Don't think.* Just go with the flow."

For what seemed like days, even though I sensed it was just minutes, all the other salmon and I swam, fished, played games, ate, and just learned to get along with one another. We did all the things that salmon do when they are young. We learned the dangers of predators and how to avoid them. We learned the safe places to feed and to rest.

I was having the time of my life. Then I noticed Sal had been right next to me the whole time. "Sal?" I asked. "I can understand my being here, but why are you here, too?"

"Oh. Well, it doesn't do any harm for an old king like me to go back to school for a little while," he said with a twinkle in his eye as he played with the rest of us. "Besides, learning has no beginning and no end."

"Hey, that looks like my best friend Randy Cole who just swam by," I told Sal. "And hey, there is Brian Benz, Philip Green, and Bryan Jackson."

I swam excitedly with each for a while, and then they would disappear, only to reappear and disappear again. I recalled that Philip had died in a car accident and how sad I had been at the loss of a friend . . . and now he was gone again.

"Why do I keep seeing my childhood friends?" I asked Sal, a bit rattled. "And why do they appear, reappear, and then disappear so quickly?"

Sal, in his all-knowing voice, answered, "You see, young Smolts, we are reliving your childhood and your school days quickly, because we are not here to visit old friends. We are here because I wanted you to see what it is like to have fun again—*what it is like to play.*"

I responded quizzically, "I think I understand—"

Sal interrupted me. "Smolts, I told you—don't think, feel. How do you *feel* when you are flowing with the school of millions of different fish swimming as one? And your old friends . . . what do you *feel* is the meaning of your seeing them again?"

I began to get the sense of what Sal was saying. *Feel. Don't think, feel.* I felt the presence of my old friends and the fun times and memories that I had with them. I would always have those memories. I loved them for being my friends and I always would, I knew. I turned slightly to face Sal, saying, "I know what this lesson is."

"Yes, young Smolts?" Sal leaned in.

"Cherish your friends and family, because they are like a salmon swimming next to you. And you never know what is going to happen, good or bad. They may be swimming by your side one day, and the next, they are gone."

"Good . . . good," is all Sal said. He was quiet for a minute and then he asked, "And why is it important to have fun . . . as a child does?"

"Let's see," I said stalling for the right answer. "It's important to have fun because . . . it keeps us young?" I blurted out.

"Hmmm . . . not bad for a guess, Smolts. Not bad." Sal responded. "You see, we need to have fun for some very important reasons. For one thing, we are all children relative to the ultimate age of the earth, and for another—as you guessed—having fun in our life does help keep our mind and body younger. But I have to explain something to you," Sal said, turning to me. "In the upcoming teachings, I am going to do my best to explain things in language that you can understand, and I may use analogies and examples from your world, such as from the sports and games that humans play."

"I see," I replied. "That will make it easier for me to understand, right?"

"Right! Now we will stay in school for a little bit longer, then we may play hooky for a day," Sal said with a slightly mischievous grin as we cruised the fabulous ocean and played in one huge wave of salmon.

Every once in a while, the school would move in sharp cuts through the water. "Why do we move like that?" I asked Sal. "And what do you mean by *playing hooky*?"

"When the school moves like that up ahead or behind us, it means the area is under attack by orcas, dolphins, or great white sharks. We move in waves to confuse the enemy, so keep a look out," he warned.

Sharks and killer whales? I thought, remembering when Sal had assured me we were safe in the massive school. "Those cute dolphins?" I asked Sal as I glanced around with much keener awareness.

"Smolts, did you forget your earlier lesson? Remember, young salmon—no guarantees!"

Suddenly a dolphin shot out of the depths at blinding speed and burst into the school, grabbing the first fish he could and quickly disappearing into the dark abyss below.

"Wow! Did you see that, Sal? Did you see that?" I screamed as I looked into the deep aquamarine ocean for signs of another predator.

"You see, you must always be on guard," Sal warned. "Even in the relative safety of this large school of fish, you must remain vigilant to the predators and dangers surrounding us. Some dangers are unavoidable, but we still want to reduce the risk of harm. Now stay tight with the school, and we will try to confuse them," Sal said in an assuring voice.

"Yes, I will," I said as I tucked in next to him. "And, I understand . . . no guarantees," I stammered in fear.

As we swam, I gained a growing awareness and appreciation of the knowledge and power that Sal possessed and was giving me. How fortunate I was to have such a great master to teach me.

But was he my master? I wondered what he meant when he said I would meet my master later and that there is no one master and yet there is only one master.

"Sal?" I asked. "What do you mean when you say I will meet my master later?"

"Oh, young Smolts, you are a curious one. You will meet your master on this journey. You will meet him," Sal repeated.

"But when?" I stubbornly asked as we pushed on. "And how will I know he is the one? And what about this *only one master* stuff?"

"Okay, Smolts," Sal said, stopping me midsentence. "If you must know, when we are done with your teachings, you will be asked to swim up the same waterfall where you almost lost your life. At the top of the falls is a series of small pools. In one of the pools, you will see your master. These pools are similar to those you stared into as a young boy."

I tried to get a feeling for what Sal was telling me. I was going to have to swim up that waterfall again? He must have confidence in me, to make me go up the falls again. *What if I fail again?* I wondered. *But I will get to meet my master when I am done.* I was confused and a little shocked.

"Hey, Sal, what if I can't make it?"

"Silence, young Smolts!" Sal snapped back at me. "I will have no talk of failure! If you fail, I have failed. I have carefully planned your training," he muttered, as if letting something slip. "We have a plan, and it is a good one," he assured me. "Always remember this: a salmon who fails to plan for what's ahead is a salmon who usually winds up dead. So you will train hard and be in the right mind and body to make it. Do you understand?"

"Yes, yes, I understand. But—"

"But what, Smolts?" Sal demanded. "What is stopping you from believing you can make it? Huh? Tell me!" he shouted.

"Well, I do have this injury and, um, I have never been successful at anything, really. And when I was a child I had to wear glasses, and . . . ," I yammered on, trying to give Sal more excuses, but he abruptly shut me off.

"Smolts! Enough! Come with me!" Sal ordered.

I followed Sal, not knowing what to expect. I was a little disappointed he wouldn't listen to all my good reasons for avoiding the dreadful falls.

As we briefly broke from the school, we swam deeper into the ocean depths. I noticed schools of different fish off in the distance. Herring or tuna maybe. It was too hard to tell. After straining more to see, my eyes were diverted below me. To my astonishment, I gazed at an amazing, long rock formation that ran across the ocean floor. It seemed to snake along like the Great Wall of China as it disappeared on each end until I could see no more.

At first it looked like a volcanic formation, but then it distinctly appeared as a wall of some type. A great divide, maybe? It was odd. One side looked as if it received direct sunlight and flourished with infinite blossoms of colorful corals and sea plants. Sea anemones swayed gracefully as if dancing with the currents. It was a plethora of colors and hues, a true sight to behold.

The other side, which received less sunlight, was dark. The only things growing were slimy green plants that buckled as the currents pushed and pulled at their grip upon the craggy rock.

"Here is the place where you can tell someone about all your reasons for failure," Sal declared. "We call it the Great Wall of Difference. This is where you can explain your problems away."

It was then that I noticed a small opening, or window, in the strange wall.

"So, go ahead, Smolts. Swim to the window and explain away," Sal ordered in a bit of a huff as he led me toward the dark side.

There were long lines of salmon on both sides of the wall. Sal and I swam down and cut right up to the window, the next salmon up seemingly glad to let Sal cut in front of him.

Well, finally! I can give all my good reasons for failure, I thought as I reached the window.

The line of salmon next to me seemed endless. "They must be other fish with injuries and problems like mine," I figured. The salmon next to me nudged me as if to announce my turn at the window. As I got there, another salmon was peering at me from the window.

He looks like me, I thought, *but a little different. But hey, so do all of them,* I remembered. "Okay, here it goes." I was ready to explain my laundry list of issues.

I described my injury, retold how my parents moved a lot, and lamented how it was hard to keep friends. I was skinny and I was not good in sports. I went on and on.

As I continued talking, the salmon across from me appeared ready to respond. So I stopped, and he butted in.

"I came from a war zone," the salmon said. "My parents died when I was only five years old. I had little food. I was sent to an orphanage. I had no friends," he continued.

Wow, I thought, *this guy really has problems.* I was stunned into silence. Then he moved aside and another salmon took his place and began to talk.

"I have a cancer that is damaging my body. My family had to sell everything just to pay for treatment."

Wow! I noticed his whole left fin was gone. I felt instant empathy for the other salmon as they continued to share their stories.

I wondered what was going on, so I swam closer and looked deep inside the window. What I saw amazed me. The line of salmon waiting to talk in the window stretched miles, farther than I could see.

Does everyone have problems like mine or worse? I wondered. *What is going on?*

"Why are these salmon telling me the reasons they failed?" I asked Sal as I turned my head back to him.

"Smolts," Sal said, "you are giving your reasons for failure, am I correct?"

"Yes, I was. That is what you told me to do," I replied, slightly annoyed.

"Yes, Smolts, I did, but you have to understand one thing. You are on the negative attitude side of the Great Wall of Difference. The other salmon are on the positive attitude side."

"What?" I asked Sal. "What do you mean? I thought you said this was a window to explain my reasons for failure."

"Yes, I did, but I did not tell you that the other side of the wall is where the salmon are telling you the reasons they've reached success in their lives, not failure! And the things they talk of are things they overcame *to be successful.*"

"What?" I stammered. "Do you mean all those salmon have been successful and have overcome all the hardships they described?"

"Yes," explained Sal, "they have all been successful at the fields they have chosen. One has earned a master's degree at age sixty-seven after eight surgeries. Another swims charity marathons with an artificial fin. Another is a veteran of the Great Orca Raid of the Andreas and uses an artificial jaw and has only one good eye," he added.

"The only difference between you and them is your attitude!" Sal said forcefully. "You have a negative attitude, and they do not. That side is the wall of *success stories*! Those things they told you were used as reasons and motivations to succeed. There is no pity given on the positive side of the wall. So the second most important thing I am going to teach you, besides always keeping your nose upstream, is to always have a positive attitude. It will carry you far and serve as a foundation for your success. Do you understand?" he asked slowly.

Although a bit embarrassed, I began to understand what Sal was talking about. When I heard what the other salmon's problems were, mine seemed like nothing in comparison. And yet, I was the one using my small problems as an excuse not to succeed, I thought sheepishly.

My gosh, I know . . . no, I feel . . . what Sal is teaching me. I have good parents, good friends, and a wife to support me. I am young and strong, with a good mind. I have what it takes to succeed. I just need to change my attitude. Time to get my head straight and realize how lucky I am, I said to myself with newfound conviction. *And I am especially lucky to have someone like Sal to teach me.*

"Sal, I have learned my lesson. From now on I will keep my nose pointed upstream and keep a positive attitude."

"Very good, young Smolts. Very good," is all Sal said. He nudged his head forward as a signal to head back to school.

10

Playing Hooky?

We swam back at a demanding pace to the large school of salmon. The swarm was picking up speed as it shimmered and flowed through the vast ocean depths. The multitude of animals and creatures I saw was awesome. Their many forms and shapes and colors made me appreciate the infinite life forms in the ocean.

What a thrill. My swim in the depths of the ocean brought forth recollections of Jacque Cousteau and his wonderful show that I remember watching as a young boy. I was living his adventures and loving it. We began swimming faster and faster, and the frantic pace snapped me out of my youthful daydream.

"Why are we going so fast?" I asked Sal, whose massive size seemed so overwhelming and yet so graceful.

"We are running hard just to strengthen our bodies and to prepare you physically for the arduous journey ahead," replied Sal. "In a short while, we will all break off into smaller groups and practice jumping and leaping. Some of you will have classes on water flow and picking out the best line in the river to swim upstream. You will partake in many classes and practice sessions," Sal responded.

"What you need to do in sales is practice your scripts, right? Practice your scripts until you know them to the point of not having to think while you use them. You will learn that your actions equal your results, and you will learn how to balance success and failure," Sal advised.

By then, I had learned not to question Sal or the routines or the classes. I just attended as many as I could. When I went to them, I went with an open mind and a good attitude . . . and I remembered to feel and to have fun.

What I learned was amazing. I learned more than I thought any fish could ever know. We had classes on what food was safe and where and how to find it. We had classes on erosion of streambeds, how to detect silt and pollution, and how to avoid it before we absorbed too much in our bodies. We jumped and we did breathing exercises for deep diving.

We had many classes on the philosophy of swimming hard. We even had classes on the meaning of important words—words that we needed to know the *true* meaning of. Words, such as *poise, patience, reverence, persistence, pride, humility, love, honor,* and *faith.* They were certainly great words . . . but they were also just empty words if you didn't understand their true meaning and absorb those meanings into your soul.

My vocabulary was growing, and so was my mind as my consciousness expanded beyond my belief. The knowledge I was obtaining was making me stronger and stronger. I was learning a lot about how to size up situations and how to make decisions that would yield the best chances of success.

"When the decision involves your conscience, the decision is yours alone," Sal would tell me. "Go with the decision that is most comfortable with your self-being, your soul," he would urge.

I looked for parallels between a salmon and a salesperson. The salesperson had to do the same types of things to stay healthy. He or she had to exercise, eat well, get good sleep, and constantly train and refresh to maintain an alert mind. The similarities were oddly amazing, I realized.

"I had no idea how much was involved in being a good salmon," I told Sal, "or a good salesperson."

"Yes, there is much involved. Much involved," he said as his voice trailed off, signaling that much was yet to be accomplished.

"So, how is your fin feeling now?" Sal asked.

I had not thought much about my injury, but it did make swimming harder. "I think I can make it," I told Sal confidently.

"Smolts, by the time we are done, the act of 'thinking you can make it' will not even cross your mind. Making it will just be the result of your efforts," he assured me.

"You will learn to use a trigger or starting point before each action," Sal continued. "This will serve as your body's notice to spring into action. From there, the thinking process will be released, allowing the subconscious mind to take over. It will guide your body from level to level without conscious interference. When you have done that, you will swim from waterfall to waterfall with little or no problem. Plan with your head, but swim with your soul," he said, but then he added, "That's one of our secrets of swimming upstream, so let's keep that between us, eh, Smolts."

"Wow, thanks Sal," I replied. "That's great info—"

"Now, I think we need a little break," Sal interrupted. "Today is hooky day! We are heading in from deep water to the mainland. Soon we will start the voyage up the great river, so today is as good a day as any to rest."

"We're going to play hooky?" I replied with a quizzical look.

"Yup." Then, with a twinkle in his eye, Sal commanded, "Follow me!" And again, we broke from the school and headed off, back into the blue ocean.

We swam for a while until I could feel the ocean becoming shallower. I noticed that it tasted different too. "Where are we going, Sal?" I asked as I struggled to keep up with the magnificent king salmon that he was. Sal swam with all the grace and power of a battleship as we headed toward the mainland. I could feel that we were entering a large bay. "Where are we, Sal?" I begged.

"You will see soon enough, young Smolts. Soon enough," Sal replied with the same grin he wore before.

As we swam along, we both picked up the distinct sounds of motors above us. Sal claimed I would eventually be able to tell what size the boats were if I stayed with him long enough. He pointed out two boats in particular and asked, "Smolts, what difference do you see between those two boats?"

By then I knew better than to ask what he meant, so I stared at each boat, closely scrutinized their shapes and sizes, and answered, "They are both fishing boats because they have lines in the water. One is going really slow. The bait he's using doesn't look like anything I'd eat. And he is trolling in an area with no fish around. The other boat has a very flashy rig and bait that looks tasty to me, and I can see that he is right above a school of salmon. He is trolling at a speed that is similar to the baitfish we chase," I outlined authoritatively.

"Very good!" Sal burst out as I finished my surveillance report. "Well, I know those boats from past trips," he claimed. "You see, a man who catches no fish is a man who comes out only occasionally and thus has no understanding of this area. The other man has maps of the terrain—even underwater maps. He studies the natural baits we eat and tries his best to imitate them. He has a fish finder, and he's an expert at using it. He knows which time of day the fish come through this area depending on the tides, moon, water temperature, and weather," he said, adding the analysis to my observations.

"But Smolts, here's the big difference," Sal asserted with his eyes staring into mine. One guy is *a fisherman*. The other man . . . he's someone who *goes fishing*. Do you get it?" he asked forcefully.

I pondered this great analogy for a few seconds. "I do! I really do," I answered. "It's just like you want to make me into a *salesman* instead of just a guy who *sells cars*."

"Great answer, Smolts. Great answer," Sal answered enthusiastically. "Now let's get going," he said as he burst into speed. "Watch out for that boat on the left," he said with a chuckle, knowing that I already knew to stay clear of the real fisherman. As we entered the bay, I noticed a shadow of a huge bridge as we swam.

Wow! That's one big bridge, I thought, because the shadow seemed to last forever until the sun broke free through the clear bay water. I could see Sal slow up as we approached the edge of the water. Sal warned me to be careful of the little boats above us as we swam to the surface to take a peek. I was getting excited because it had been a while since I had looked above the waterline.

My head broke the water. My fish eyes gazed in wonder at what surrounded me. A large waterfront was on the left, with tall buildings behind it. I turned to my right and saw what we had come up for. Just about that time I heard a loud, windy roar! Sal yelled, "Look out!"

Out of the corner of my eye, I could see a baseball flying down almost straight at us. "Duck!" Sal yelled, as he dove below the surface.

I stayed up just in time to see two kayaks paddling frantically toward me. "Ahhh!" I screamed, and I ducked below the waves, barely being missed by the baseball and a big net that a man in one of the kayaks was using in hopes of snagging the ball.

"Sal! You brought me to a big-league baseball game in the park by the bay!" I yelled in joy. I swam around and poked my head up again. This was a strange view, but one I would never forget. I stared up at the huge white wall and pillars of the great San Francisco ballpark. The crowd roared and booed on each pitch and swing.

I glanced over to Sal and I could see a face of contentment as he gazed up at the magnificent ballpark.

"She is a beauty," he said, "a real beauty." After a while, Sal broke his silence and swam over to me. "There is another reason I brought you here, young Smolts."

"It's *Deyoung* Smolts, Sal, Deyoung," I said, slightly annoyed. "Why do you keep calling me *young Smolts*—and what other reason are you talking about?" I inquired.

"You told me that you wanted to sell only the cars with the big profit in them and that other sales were a waste of time, especially the ones you split the commission on," Sal recalled. "Am I right?"

I did remember saying that, so I answered honestly, "Yeah, Sal, I would just like to sell the cars with the most profit. Is that wrong?"

"Yes, it is wrong," Sal asserted, "and that is why we are here. I am going to show you why you need to sell all types of deals to all types of customers. And I am going to use baseball to do it," he claimed with that self-assured tone I had heard before.

"Baseball?" I countered. "How are you going to do that?"

"Let me ask you, young Smolts, what makes a Hall of Fame baseball player?"

With the distinct feeling that I was being set up, I reluctantly answered as I rolled my fish eyes. "Well, okay, Sal. How about one that can hit a lot of home runs and play good defense and get clutch hits . . . one who hits for a high average." As I began to see what Sal was getting at, I added, "Uh, and one who plays hard."

"Right. Most of the players you see out there today can play great offense. They hit the ball hard and they have good averages. What is your job, young Smolts?" he asked pointedly.

"My job? To sell a car! You know that . . . I already told you, Sal." My patience was wearing thin at this little game of his.

"Wrong," Sal shot back. "If I remember, your job is to get a proposal up to the management so they can put the deal together. Am I right?"

"Well, yeah, you're right, but I am getting good at knowing what trades are worth and what new cars cost," I replied, adding, "so I know what payments—"

"Stop! Does a baseball player try to manage the game for his coach?" Sal asked forcefully. "Or does he just try to hit the ball *every time*?" Sal hammered.

I knew this was a trick question. But I knew I had him this time, because I remembered something from my old baseball coach. "Sal, a good ballplayer just tries to hit the ball as hard and cleanly as he can; then he runs out the play as well as he can," I offered.

"Why do you feel he does that?" Sal responded, barely giving me breathing room to think.

"He does that because it's all he can control," I answered. "Too many things can happen during play that he can't control."

"And how does that differ from your job?" Sal asked with a lowered voice and tone.

Now I knew what Sal had done. He *had* set me up. The jobs were no different. I should just be helping each customer the best I can, getting the best proposal I can, and submitting it to the manager. "You're right, Sal!" I asked. "But how do you know so much about the auto business?"

I caught him off guard. "Uhh," he stammered, "let's just say I had a good teacher . . ." as his voice trailed off. "Now, don't ask silly questions," he said, obviously changing the subject back. "Now you are prepared. Your attitude and effort, those are the things you can control. And you need every deal to get your averages so you can become a great salesperson, just as a great baseball player works," Sal claimed. "The difference between being an all-star and being sent to AAA could be a couple of run-out singles in a meaningless game. And I believe you would have won top salesman if you had stayed on task and not let other people split some deals you had already closed. That is what I am talking about. You need every write-up and every sale," Sal lectured.

Sal has his ways, I said to myself as I soaked in the valuable insight.

He looked at me with praise and inquired, "So we have now talked about what makes a good offensive player, but what about defense? Doesn't defense make a complete player?"

"Defense?" I responded.

"Yes," Sal said emphatically. "That's what makes a well-rounded player. I know everyone wants to hit the ball, but not everyone wants to practice defense. But it's the player who hits for average and plays great defense who gets the invitation to the All-Star Game."

"But how can I compare the baseball player who plays good defense to my auto sales job?" I asked.

"I will show you," Sal said. "Try to follow me on this one. Everyone wants to sell cars to people who walk in and ask for a salesperson . . . am I right?"

"Yes, that is where most sales are made. We call them fresh ups," I told him.

"Well, you are wrong, young Smolts. Believe it or not, I happen to know what the national averages are for auto sales in this country. And by using them, and by learning how a salesperson plays defense, you will learn how to be a top producer," Sal asserted.

He continued, "Now a good salesperson sells about eighteen out of one hundred fresh ups that he or she will see. And most salespeople see only about fifty ups a month. So, if a salesperson is lucky, he will sell seven to eight vehicles a month from the floor ups . . . are you following me?" Sal asked as I became increasingly curious how a hundred-pound king salmon knew so much about new auto sales.

"Yes," I said, "but I sold eleven cars my first month. All from fresh ups," I told him, "and eight the next."

"And how many the third month?" he pressed.

"What? The third month? Oh, four, I think"

"And how many does that average?" Sal asked.

"Okay, okay. So what's your point?" I asked him.

"My point, Smolts, is that you have been playing only offense. Defense in baseball is like appointments in auto sales."

"Appointments?" I asked impatiently. "They are hard to get. And I—"

"Nonsense!" Sal snapped at me. "It's like the ball player who doesn't want to play defense. But fifty percent of customers buy a vehicle if they come in and ask for you by name or otherwise have an appointment with you."

"Fifty percent? Are you kidding?" I asked with surprise, wondering how he knew that and I did not.

"So using the baseball player's law of averages, if you get fifty ups a month and fifteen appointments, you should sell fifteen cars a month on average. Do you understand?" Sal pushed.

"Yes, I believe so. I didn't realize until now how important appointments were, Sal. But, still, they are hard to make."

"Not so! Nothing you do will be as hard as what you are going through today. All you need is a plan to make more appointments and then work the plan with a positive attitude. When you get back to school, we will set you up with some classes on selling skills, scripts for every situation, phone skills, appointment setting, and a good follow-up system to track and sell your previous clients. You will do a complete spring training on auto sales. Eh, Smolts?" Sal said with conviction in his voice. I sensed he felt we were getting somewhere.

"So. What have you learned?" Sal asked as he indicated it was time to go.

"Oh, I learned a ton," I assured Sal, "and I had fun doing it. I will now use the averages to better my percentages of success. That is what I am going to do. And play defense, too!"

"You are learning, young Smolts. You are learning," Sal concluded.

The baseball game was great, but it came to a sudden end. We took one last peek and reluctantly turned back toward the open sea to make the swim back to school.

11

A Blind Salmon?

The swim back to the salmon swarm did not take long because the large school had worked its way closer to the mainland. Just as we arrived, all the fish began to separate into smaller groups. I learned they would soon head out alone up the rivers and streams that dotted the coastline.

"Some of these salmon will never see their friends again, will they?" I asked Sal.

"No, they won't," answered Sal. "It is similar to when you humans break out of high school and continue your education in smaller groups as you work toward adulthood."

It was then that I realized I might never see some of the friends I had made at Sal's training and felt instant loss. "I understand, Sal," I replied. "So we have learned the basics, right, and now we will go on to learn skills and philosophies that will take us to the next level?"

"Yes, Smolts! Yes," Sal answered, obviously happy that I was starting to pick up the whole plan that he had for me, to relearn what I had forgotten . . . and more.

We swam up to the school just in time to say my last good-byes to the friends I had made. I would likely see some of them on my journey, but I was just as sure I would never see many others.

The good-byes were short and somewhat ill at ease, but still heart-felt, as we prepared to take the next step.

"Where do we go from here?" I asked Sal as the small group we joined headed for the coast.

"We are looking for the mouth of the great river," Sal told me.

"Is it the river we came from? How will we know where it is?" I asked Sal.

"We will know," is all Sal said.

We picked up speed and charged ahead. The smaller group of about two hundred thousand salmon, including Sal and me, were swimming along at an easy pace, when suddenly the whole school lurched sideways and cut for deeper water. Sal and I instantly sensed danger as we followed the group.

Whoooooosh! It was the sound of a large fishing net as it lurched fifty feet above us, scooping up hundreds of helpless, writhing salmon.

"Sal, is there nothing we can do?" I screamed as we dove deeper into the ocean.

"We can do nothing. Death is part of life," Sal said with a calm and matter-of-fact tone.

As we continued swimming on, I pondered the ultimate fate of the salmon caught in the net. I wondered if any of my new friends were in there.

"Where do we go from here?" I asked as our school slowed, now out of the danger of the fishing nets.

"We will soon start up the mouth of the river," Sal said. "There you will get some of the special training I spoke of," he added. "After you are done, we will start to head upriver and eventually get to the spot where you will be tested."

I had to ask Sal the ultimate salmon question. "Sal, how do salmon know how to travel the vast ocean and find the exact river where they must begin their journey?"

"That is an easy one," Sal answered with a big smile. "We

know the path!" And with a flick of his tail, he got up a burst of speed and took off laughing in front of me.

"You know the path, huh? That's not funny, Sal!" I yelled as I worked frantically to catch up with him. By the time I reached him, I was too tired to press on with my questioning and I could feel the school slow again and settle into a holding pattern.

"Are we here?" I asked Sal. I could feel the excitement in the water as the other salmon prepared to go forward.

"We are here," Sal said.

"Well, I'm ready!" I exclaimed. "I have taken the right classes. I have a good attitude. I am going to give it a hundred and ten percent. I am ready!

"A hundred and ten percent? Why not a hundred and twenty percent?" Sal asked with stone-faced seriousness.

"Uh, okay, a hundred and twenty percent," I said with a little less enthusiasm.

"Why not a hundred and fifty percent, young Smolts?" Sal pressed.

It seemed like I was in trouble. *What did I do?* I thought. "Okay, a hundred and fifty."

And before I could say anything else, Sal interrupted. "Enough of this nonsense! There is nothing over a hundred percent effort . . . period! Otherwise, we could go to a thousand percent. Do you understand?" he asserted.

"Okay, I understand," I shot back as I realized the simplicity of what he was saying.

Sal continued his rant. "It is the desire that creates aptitude. Persistence. Perseverance. Intestinal fortitude—all things you should know—"

I cut him off. "Can a person be giving a hundred percent effort all the time, Sal?" I asked out of curiosity. "Wouldn't that person burn out?"

"No. You see, a salmon gives a hundred percent effort everyday to survive his two-thousand-mile journey of life, just as a human must do," Sal said after calming down. "Then you break it down to everyday life and activities, even the sports you play. Like the pro golfers you like to watch on television. They set a pace of play. They give a hundred percent effort to keeping that pace, while breaking it all the way down to envisioning each shot and giving a hundred percent effort to execute it, from their preshot routine, their shots, and their follow-through. Then the golfer may relax and replenish his body in between, giving a hundred percent to doing that. He has an ultimate goal in mind, like you do. But his concentration is not on what has happened in the past, or on what score he ends up with at the end of the round . . . but on what is happening *right now*!" Sal added, as I again wondered how he knew so much about the human world.

"Then, when the golfer is done with the tournament, he may go home and give one hundred percent to his wife and children. Do you see what I am getting at, young Smolts?"

"Yes," I told Sal. "By giving one hundred percent everyday, whatever you are doing should be done with conviction and meaning and purpose."

"Indeed!" Sal agreed. "Of course, one hundred percent will vary depending on whether you are healthy or sick." Then he hesitated for a second and said, "Remember, when you give one hundred percent, you avoid self-judgment and regret. And always remember: when we face the river head-on, we become stronger," he reminded me.

"Now, before we head off to the great river, I want you to know that the great river never brings down challenges that are beyond your ability to handle, although you may wonder at the time how you will succeed. I have learned that when the river brings you these challenges, the easier stretch of river is usually right around the bend," Sal advised in a tone that resounded of past experiences.

He hesitated for just a second, and then he added in a very serious tone, "Young Smolts, a matter of critical importance must be discussed."

"What?" I answered, hanging on his every syllable.

"You must be committed to make it as far as you can. Committed to swimming hard until your last breath. A true commitment," he warned. "I am talking about something sacred. A *salmon commitment,*" he stated proudly.

"A salmon commitment?" I asked. "What is that?"

"Well, a salmon commitment comes from an old folk story in our world," Sal replied. "It is a wonderful story and I want you to listen carefully for the lessons within it."

"Okay," I agreed, paying full attention because I was still curious about that salmon commitment thing.

"There was once a salmon," Sal said as he slowed up slightly, "who had become landlocked in a farmer's pond after a huge flood. The farmer came out after the flood and noticed the salmon in his pond. Instead of killing the salmon, the farmer fed him, and let him stay in the pond as long as he wished.

"Months later a chicken, who had befriended the salmon, told him that the farmer's fiftieth birthday was the following day. They wanted badly to give the farmer the best present they could. But having no money, they could buy him nothing. After much thought, a grand breakfast was planned for the farmer," Sal continued as listened closely.

"Well, the next morning the farmer woke to find fresh grilled salmon fillet and scrambled eggs waiting on the kitchen table, served up just the way he liked them," Sal said.

All I could do was just stare at Sal, confused. Then he continued.

"You see, it is said that the chicken was *involved* in giving the farmer a great breakfast, but the salmon was *committed.* Do you see the point of the story, young Smolts?"

I was in shock and could only stammer, "Do you mean I have

to be *willing to die*? Is that what you're telling me?" I replied in disbelief.

"Well, in a nonphysical sense, yes," Sal replied. "Besides, if you are not committed to life and to living it to the best of your abilities, then you are not living fully," he added. "Let me ask you something, Smolts," he suddenly said. "When you were catching me, how committed were you?"

My mind flashed back to the fight of my life on the river earlier. "Well, I was ready to do almost anything to catch you, Sal," I recalled. "In fact, as I remember, I almost died under the water."

"Now you see, Smolts—commitment!" Sal said with a big smile. He knew he had given me the perfect example. Then Sal added in a serious tone, "I want to mention something else before we head upstream."

"What's that?" I asked.

"We will all see many different variables as we enter the stream of life, and we will all encounter many various water conditions as we swim onward—some good, some bad, and many in-between," he described in that teacher-like tone of his.

"There are times to follow a path, times the path is decided for you, and times you will swim your own path. Sometimes you may even face paths that demand you turn back and start again in an alternate direction," he continued.

"Well, wouldn't that be going backward?" I asked sheepishly.

He seemed to sense my hesitation. "Never be afraid to ask any questions, Smolts," he shot back emphatically. "No. That is not going backward," Sal asserted. "There is a difference between knowing the course and swimming the course. That is where your commitment comes in. Sometimes you may properly execute the wrong move and find yourself having to go back just to go forward. So as long as you are focused, with a clear mind and commitment, then you are mentally headed in the right direction and you are making the best of the situation. In short, your nose is pointed upstream."

With that explanation, I began to understand the philosophy of forward thinking and why it is important to keep moving forward with a positive attitude.

"Yes, admit the failures," Sal blurted out. "Make the changes so as not to repeat the failure . . . *and then keep swimming*. Whatever the situation, continuing to swim helps you wallow in the quagmire," he added.

Wallow in the quagmire? "What do you mean, wallow in the quagmire? What quagmire?" I asked in frustration.

I could tell as he slowed that he was back in that philosopher role again. "A *quagmire* is a multitude of conditions that you will encounter in your life. It is like a stagnant pond, full of life. What I mean is, wherever you are, immerse yourself in the situation and then use the surroundings and the situation to your benefit. Do you understand me?" he asked.

"Yes! I do. Well, I think I do," I stammered back. "It sounds like when I played high school football. We never cared if it rained or if it was hot or if the field was muddy or whatever. The real football players just wanted to play! We wallowed in that quagmire!"

"Yes, you can say you did, young Smolts. You can say you did," Sal laughed. "Now, it is almost our turn to head up the great river, so get ready," Sal urged.

As the school dispersed farther up, we made our way toward the mouth of the river. The water tasted clean again as we swam into the large inlet of fresh, clear water. I noticed that my fin had not quite healed. I tried not to let Sal sense my worry as I forged ahead.

"Smolts!" Sal called to me. "I see you are still worried about your fin, so I am going to have another master work with you today while I help some other salmon," he announced.

"My fin is fine!" I shot back stubbornly. "So who's *this* master and what's *he* going to teach me?"

Sal looked at me and merely tilted his head. I followed. Off in the distance I could see an older salmon by the entrance to the river. He looked as if he could barely move as he floated almost motionless. His eyes looked white and glazed over, almost scary.

"Is that the salmon that is going to teach me?" I asked Sal with some doubtfulness in my breath.

"Yes," replied Sal, "that is Master Cohosaki, and he is blind."

"Blind! What?" I asked. "Who is Master Cohosaki? Where is he from? And what am I supposed to learn from an old blind fish?"

"Silence, young Smolts!" Sal blurted. "I will hear none of that! Remember—empty your cup! We are lucky to have Master Cohosaki visiting from the Orient. He is a true master, and he is here to teach you the ways of the great river. Is that clear?" Sal added firmly.

"Yes, Sal, I'm sorry. I will never question you again." I knew very well not to question Sal, especially after all he had done for me and taught me so far.

We approached Master Cohosaki from the back and swam up to meet him.

Before we could speak, the master calmly said, "Sal, how are you, my friend! I see you have a young Smolts for me to train."

I was stunned. How did he know my name and how did he know Sal and I were even there?

"Yes, Coho! Good to see you, old friend," Sal replied warmly. "It has been too long, no?"

"So, Sal, why do you bring me this one?" The master asked.

"He has a fin injury and he thinks it may hamper him on his journey upriver. But he is here to learn whatever he needs," Sal replied.

"I see. Very well," Master Cohosaki answered. "Leave him

with me, and we will meet back here when he is ready, just as before."

I moved slowly in the water, shocked that Sal was leaving and that Master Cohosaki knew so much already. I wondered how. "I'll be back soon," Sal uttered faintly as he turned his great body and swam back in the direction from which we had arrived.

"I don't know what to say," I stammered as I tried to talk to the blind fish.

"You do not have to say much, young Smolts," Master Cohosaki answered. "You just have to listen and learn and use the lessons that Sal and others have taught you."

"I thought I learned what I needed out in the ocean," I replied.

"Yes, but you did not learn what you need to know to get you up the great river. That is what I am here for. Come with me," he commanded. With a kick of his tail, he took off more quickly than I expected and headed toward the mouth of the river.

As we entered the river, I could feel the cool, clear water run through me like a breath of fresh air. I was starting to get confident in my abilities, and I could feel my head swell.

"When I am off on my own, I will be free!" I asserted boldly to Master Cohosaki. "I will have learned everything, and life will be so easy and great for me!"

Master Cohosaki did not say anything at first, but then he slowly mumbled, "Always the illusion of an easy path, always the illusion," his voice trailing off.

Suddenly he turned to face me. It was amazing, his eyes were glazed over, but it looked as if he was staring right into my soul. Then he stated. "Remember this: freedom is a born right, but not always a given one. Relish being free. You are a chosen one," he asserted strongly.

That was strong, I thought, as his mystic glaze broke mine and he kept swimming and talking.

"If my memory serves me correctly, young Smolts, in your

human world you, too, had a great king." He said *king* with a special tone and look that showed he was referring to his race of king salmon. "His name was Martin Luther King, and he once said, 'With great freedom, comes great responsibility.' *Great responsibility.* Young Smolts, I want you to absorb those words into your soul and believe them. Live them," Cohosaki urged.

"And the easy path? That is always the course upon which to be most careful, my friend, always the one," he reiterated, his voice again trailing off so I could barely hear his last word. But just the tone of Master Cohosaki's voice let me know how serious he was. The path was never going to be easy. And never, and I mean never, would I take my freedom for granted again. Then Master Cohosaki went back to some basic training and I listened intently.

"Always remember this, Smolts. Always keep your tail moving forward. When you are in the great river, the water flow is constant, and so must be your effort," he warned. "You see, the flow can change from what you think is quiet stillness to a relentless force at a moment's notice. The number one rule is always keep moving with your nose pointed upstream. Pay attention to what is directly ahead or you may wind up dead," he warned.

"Yes, I learned about the nose upstream part," I told him. "But I did not know we had to keep moving all the time."

"I mean it literally for us salmon. But when you are a human again, understand you must always be moving forward, hence *forward thinking.* Salmon in the river know if they stay still or turn sideways, the current will grab them and take them downstream. No one wants to go backward, eh, my young Smolts?" Cohosaki pressed.

"I understand," I answered. "If you are not moving forward, then you might as well be going backward."

"Yes. You can say that," Master Cohosaki said with a small laugh. "You can say that, indeed."

Master Cohosaki then asked, "Young Smolts, why do you hate this Jeff person you work with?"

"What?" I blurted. His question really caught me off guard. How'd he know about Jeff?

"Jeff? At work? Oh, that jerk. Man, I tell you, he is always bugging me and telling me I am not very good. And he outsells me . . . and—"

"Stop! Stop, young Smolts. *Hate* is a powerful word. I cannot tell you what to feel. But if I can borrow from the great Dr. King again: 'Let no man pull you low enough to hate him.' These are words you can live by," Cohosaki urged. "Also, don't take anything personally. Nothing others do is because of you. What they do and say to you is a projection of them, not you. When you are immune to the opinions and actions of others, you will not be the victim you think you are. Besides, we all have some people who like us or don't like us. It is an unavoidable projection of their soul, their being . . . and again, not yours," the master asserted.

Let no man pull you low enough to hate him, and don't be the victim, I repeated in my head. *Wow! Truly wise words,* I thought to myself.

Master Cohosaki and I worked our way up the center of the river a few miles until the river began to narrow, talking and practicing and having a little fun along the way.

He talked to me about love. "Don't be afraid to love," he urged. "Telling friends you love them is a gift."

"What is love?" I asked, wondering as I have for many years just what that concept really means.

He pondered for just a moment, and then he answered. "An understanding," is all he said, and then he settled into a deep, trance-like silence.

I began to look at him in awe and wonder. It did not seem that he was actually blind. He was a red-gray color, unlike Sal and me, way smaller then Sal, maybe forty pounds. But he swam effortlessly and cut and weaved around obstacles with little effort. When a morsel of food would float by, he would snatch it in a flash with little wasted effort. He was something to behold.

As we slowed, I could tell we were reaching our destination. I spotted a large, slow pool below some small falls.

"Here is where we will train, young Smolts," the master said as he stopped swimming. "Now, young Smolts, close your eyes and tell me what you hear."

"What I hear?" I asked, clearly puzzled.

"Yes. What do you hear?" Master Cohosaki repeated.

I was curious about what the master wanted to know, so I closed my eyes and listened. "I hear the water flowing down the falls," I replied. "I hear a fishing boat behind us. And I hear a shore bird in the distance," I proudly answered.

"Is that all?" Master Cohosaki asked pointedly.

I strained again to hear something else . . . anything . . . nothing. "Nope, that's it," I answered.

"Do you hear the eagle resting on the branch on the tall redwood by the shore? Do you hear the fox as it scrounges for mice on the bank? Do you hear your heartbeat? Do you hear the hellgrammite as it digs under the small, gray rock below you?" the master pressed.

No way! I thought as I swam up to the surface to take a look. *Eagle in a tree, my tail!* But then I spotted a bald eagle perched on a towering redwood at least a hundred feet up the trunk. I turned to my right and caught a red-tailed fox bouncing out from behind some bushes, only to be scared back as the eagle spotted us and flew off his perch and headed toward us.

I'm out of here! I said to myself. I'd had my share of eagles today—I quickly dove back to deeper water.

I swam past Master Cohosaki to a small gray rock that glistened from the sun's reflection. I flipped it over with my nose and there it was. A large, black hellgrammite. It was a good three inches long, with big pinchers on its tail and lots of legs. The force of the rock flipping over caused enough turbulence to flush out whatever lay beneath. It rolled up into a ball and tumbled up toward me.

By instinct, I snatched it with my mouth and gulped it down. *Did I just eat that nasty thing?* I asked myself in disbelief.

"You did at that, " Cohosaki replied, bursting into laughter. "You did at that."

As he settled down, I asked him, "Master, how is it that you can hear all these things?"

"Young Smolts, how is it that you cannot?" With that statement, he turned toward an area by the falls that looked like an obstacle course. I quickly followed, as I tried my best to remember all this wonderful knowledge, and he began to talk.

"Young Smolts, you have to understand that we are not bound by any limits. When I was young, I lost my sight from a chemical spill. I was forced to make a choice—a choice to wither away or use the senses I have left to live. I chose to live."

" I found, even with closed eyes, one can see, but with a closed mind, one cannot "

Then he stopped and turned to me. "Deyoung, in your world of sales, you, too, have a step you must explore and go beyond."

"A step beyond?" I asked. I was fixated on what he was telling me.

"Yes, a step beyond," Master Cohosaki said. "You have to learn the psychology of selling. What type of person are you dealing with? What is his or her motivation? What are his true objections, her wants and needs? Then you must master numerous closing techniques at your disposal. Just think. Does your great country have just one or two ships or bombers when its forces go to war?" he asked.

"No. They have every type of weapon they can find, plus some. And espionage and counter-intelligence. But I am not in a war at work," I replied.

"Yes, you are: a psychological war. That is the way you have to look at it," Cohosaki asserted. "You must have everything at your disposal, because you never know what the great river of life will bring down on you, or what a customer will do or say. Now, today we will learn new techniques and styles, and you will practice them until you know them like the back of your fin. We will concentrate on your damaged fin so it will become a strength and not a weakness," he added. I was thankful to hear that.

"But how will I know which style is going to work best for me, Master?" I asked.

"Your style? Learn *all styles,* Smolts, because you do not want to limit the style in which one sells or lives because you never know what life—or a customer—will throw at you," the master urged. "When you greet a new client, you never really know what you are going to be up against when you try to sell them. Just as we salmon never ever know what is coming down upon us from the river above. Be prepared. Learn all styles that can be used in as many situations as you can. Doing so will benefit you greatly," he urged, " but we need to get back to your training now."

"You will learn to stay healthy and fit by eating the right food and doing the right exercises," he outlined. "You will be given a schedule of future training so your skills can be continually sharpened and refined. And you will be taught how to sharpen all your senses so you can almost see things before they happen. *You will be taught to be like water*." Master Cohosaki said mysteriously.

"Be like water?" I asked, wondering what he was hitting me with now.

"Yes," Master Cohosaki went on to explain. "There was a great grand master named Bruce Lee, who lived among your people. He put it like this, if I can remember it correctly: 'You put water into a jar, it becomes the jar. You put water into a teapot, it becomes the teapot. Water is soft, yet it can freeze and turn to ice. It can become a glacier that moves mountains. It can turn to steam and power a great train, or it can come down with enough force to wash away a city.' Be like water my friend. Be like water," the master implored.

I remembered Bruce Lee's movies. I loved them. How smart Cohosaki was, I thought, as I swam almost motionless. I absorbed the valuable insights that were being offered to me. I had already learned a lot. But I knew there was more to come.

"Are you ready?" Master Cohosaki asked.

I snapped to and shouted with renewed enthusiasm, "I am ready!"

Suddenly, and innocently, I asked him, "Do you have psychic powers? Is that how you get around?"

At first he was quiet, surprised at my question. But with a light chuckle he answered, "No, young Smolts. I just . . . ," he said, his voice stalling a little, "I just pay attention to the details," he added curtly.

And with those words of confidence, he swam onward. He must surely be the master I will meet in the pool above the falls, I thought to myself. Master Cohosaki then made a motion to get started.

The day seemed to last forever as the master not only trained me physically but also trained my mind. He taught me things such as sensory perception, body language, and changing the tone and inflection in my speech. He helped me paint a mental picture of success, breaking it all down, step by step. He showed me how activity and your attitude about it will get you the results, all things that would make a huge difference in my success in sales and in life. *This is awesome,* I kept thinking.

But I had some minor failures. One time I failed to make it up a set of rapids, and I began blurting out an excuse as to why I did not make it. But before I could get one word out, the master cut me off.

"No excuses, young Smolts," he warned. "Have reasons for

your failings, *but not excuses*. Adjust to the conditions of the failure and be determined to succeed on the next run."

He had me swim up the small falls, over and over, again and again.

"Practice to the point where you will be able to swim without the burden of thought," he kept saying. "Take ownership of yourself . . . *be the water*."

I practiced until a slow but sudden transformation took over me. All of me—my mind, my body, my self, and my soul. I came to a point where I could not just see where to go, but I could *feel* where to go. I began tracking up the waterfalls with a newfound ease. It was a freedom I had never sensed before! I was flashing in and out of temporary zones where my body just took over and carried me from level to level. Then I would flash back and I would struggle for a while. Occasionally Master Cohosaki would yell out to me.

"It is the action that leads to the result! Be quick and clean. See the path, be the path. Rush, but don't hurry. Don't think, *feeeeel*," he urged. "Have options—two or three or even four, if needed. Find the way. Capture the momentum! Ride it as long as you can," he added enthusiastically.

Whenever I got to the point of total exhaustion, he would say, "Rest if you need to, but minimize your movement, your energy. Remove the burden of thought!"

Repeatedly, I would go up the falls and be pushed back down. He would have me go again and I could hear him yell, "Be like a boxer: Two steps forward, one back. Three forward, one back. You get knocked down; you get up and go forward. Take calculated risks. Ask yourself, 'What could happen? What is affected? Is it the best time? Are there less risky options?'"

Continually, I could hear Cohosaki call out, "Make the transition from one waterfall to the next. Make it seamless, seamless. Swim strong, swim strong . . . always swim strong!"

One time he stopped me for a moment with some extra advice. "Smolts, learn to explore yourself internally," he said. "Integrate yourself into your being."

It was really amazing as the extra training transformed me from young, scared Smolts to a strong, young fighter. Time seemed to fly by as my training took me to new heights of awareness and ability. I was saddened when the great master told me we were almost done. My body swelled with newfound confidence, and I felt like I had just spent a lifetime with a martial arts master at a Buddhist monastery. I could do, feel, and see things that I never thought I would be capable of. I was fast becoming my own salmon. And I liked being my own salmon. As the session came to an end, I swam up to Master Cohosaki and gleefully told him, "I am stronger and smarter now. I will make it up the river!"

"Yes, you have done well, young Smolts," Master Cohosaki said. "But there is one more thing I want you to learn before we go. Something I want you to understand: do not get caught up in counting your victories and defeats," he said guardedly.

"Why is that, Master?" I asked.

"Because some defeats end up being victories, and some victories end up being defeats," he warned.

"How is that so?" I tried to follow him.

"For example, young Smolts, remember when you caught the carp?" he asked.

"Yes, it was terrible," I replied.

"And then you bent one of your hooks and made it weak," he said, as if he had been there. "Is that correct?"

"Yes, that's how it happened," I answered.

"And then when you cast—your last cast of the day—did not the wind blow the lure into the rapids of the waterfall?" he pressed.

"Yes, that was really bad. But how did you ...?" I began to ask, and then I figured it was no use as I rambled on. "Well . . . yes, it was the worst luck. My hook almost broke while trying to bend it back, and then my lure got stuck . . . and then—" I stammered.

"Yes, that was unfortunate at the time," he interrupted. "But didn't you catch Sal in the falls? And did not the bent hook allow you to free Sal from the old tree in the water?"

"What? Why, yes it did!" I responded. "So it was really lucky that I caught the carp and bent the hook. Hey, I see where you are going with this. Sometimes defeats are victories in disguise. That is why staying positive is a must . . . but why can't I celebrate the victories?"

"Because the victories are not always victories," he answered. "Do you remember when you sold the 'clearance' car for a seven hundred fifty dollar minimum commission last month, and you bragged to everyone and went out and blew the money?" the master asked.

"Uh, yes I do. The deal rolled back because they could not get it financed, and I wound up getting nothing. I was a head case for the rest of the month. I didn't hit my minimum sales quota. I see what you are teaching me," I admitted.

"Do your best to stay on an even keel through the victories and the defeats," I said, recasting what he was telling me. "And it is best to stay somewhat humble."

"Very good, young Smolts, very good," Master Cohosaki replied. "Always remember, a humble pie is still a good pie."

"A humble pie is still a good pie?" I repeated.

"You see, young Smolts, to a man starved of humbleness, a humble pie is the best-tasting pie he can eat," he explained. "For a good man, that is why humble pie makes a great dessert.

"Always remember," he continued, "let your actions speak for you. A good salesman brags, but great salesmen let their sales brag for them. Also, when you speak, speak with integrity. Say only what you mean. Don't gossip, and don't beat yourself up!"

"Humble pie is a good pie, and speak with integrity," I recited to myself. I got the picture he was painting. You are never sure of success or failure. So stay humble. As Sal said, there are no guarantees. But why, I wondered, and I innocently asked, "So why are there no guarantees?"

"Oh, there is one guarantee, young Smolts. There is one guarantee. If you keep your nose pointed upstream, keep a positive attitude, and give one hundred percent everyday, your chances of obtaining success rise greatly. That is guaranteed," he assured me.

Master Cohosaki announced that my lessons were now over. It was time to go, and I was ready.

"Any last words of advice?" I asked innocently.

"Yes," he answered, as if he had pondered the timing of my question. "In your journey upstream, the highest achievement of technique is to have no technique," he said, leaving me a little puzzled yet again. "Like the shadow that follows you on the river floor—it moves with you. It becomes you. Its movements are a result of yours. When you have reached true awareness, you will be formless, like a drop of rain as it hits the water above. It instantly dissipates into the water. It *becomes* the water. When you have reached the level of having no forms, then you can be *all* forms. I wish you the fortune of someday obtaining that level of awareness," he concluded with a loving smile.

I swam there motionless, in utter awe of his grand wisdom.

"It is now time to go," he announced, snapping me out of my temporary trance.

"Wait!" I told him as I felt something nearby. "Hold on a second," and with a burst of my tail, I dove deep into the clear water and headed toward a small rock. I quickly flipped it over and a tasty hellgrammite gently rolled up into the water flow. I quickly gulped it down, and with a kick of my tail, I swam back to Master Cohosaki, yelling, "Didn't want to waste a good meal!"

12

Shiny Rocks!

As Cohosaki and I said our last good-byes, I made sure to pay my respects to this great master. He had taught me more than I could have possibly dreamed of. There would be a next level in my life, and a next, just as in the salmon's journey up the great river.

And it would be up to me to do whatever it took to make it to those levels. With my new skills and attitude, I knew my chances of success had greatly increased.

"Thank you, great Master Cohosaki," I told him appreciatively. "Thank you, and I—" but he gave me a nod that suggested I stop talking.

"You are welcome, young Smolts. You are truly welcome," he proudly said. "But the best way to thank me is through your future actions. Let me see a consistent and sincere effort from you, an effort to use these lessons to help you . . . and your family. Never feel that what you have learned entitles you to anything," he cautioned, but then he added, "Expected entitlement and habits are death in our world. Remember, young Smolts—be the message that you send."

I understood—*and felt*—what he said. If you're going to talk the talk, you better walk the walk ... or swim the swim. But "be the message that you send" was a way cooler way to put it, that was for sure.

So against his objections, I thanked him again.

"Young Smolts," Master Cohosaki interrupted, "close your eyes and tell me what you hear."

I knew this drill by now, so I closed my eyes and listened. "I hear the waterfall, the bubbles rising to the surface; I hear a school of two- or three-pound largemouth bass, about seven or eight of them seeking cover in the branches from the sunken tree on our left. I hear a crawdad building a nest below. I hear my heartbeat . . . and I can hear yours!" I proudly declared.

For a moment we both swam side by side, our noses pointed upstream, our hearts beating as one. I felt majestic. Self-assured. Confident. At peace. For the first time in a long time.

Suddenly I blurted out, "I can hear . . . it's Sal!" I turned around to see my mentor and friend swimming up behind us. He was still about sixty feet back and a much smaller salmon was trailing him.

With a burst of my tail, I set out to greet him. "Sal! How are you?" I shouted.

Sal, obviously happy to see me too, shouted back. "Smolts! I am doing well! And I see by your new sculpted body that you are doing well, too."

"I am doing fabulously. You would not believe what a great teacher Master Cohosaki is, Sal." Then I backed down a little because Sal obviously did know.

"We did everything, and—"

Sal interrupted. "Coho, old friend, how are you!" as Master Cohosaki silently swam up behind me.

"Sal, I am great," he said. "This one you brought me is quite a feisty one. But strong and determined."

"He is at that. He is at that," Sal said with a little chuckle and a look of pride.

As they swam off to talk, I could overhear them a little.

"He is a fine young salmon," I heard Master Cohosaki say. "He may be a master one day himself if he stays focused," he added.

But Cohosaki then made a motion to another salmon I did not know that was waiting off to the side. I thought I heard him say, "Another young Smolts, eh?" and utter a little chuckle.

Both Sal and Master Cohosaki turned serious for a moment. "Until we swim side by side in the great river again, my friend," Sal said to him. Then the strangest sound came out of Sal's mouth. It had a high pitch. I strained to decipher, but I can only describe it as "Squuii ubieii yiie leee bweeee." It threw me off for a second. It was then that Sal gave one last quick nod to Master Cohosaki as a final good-bye.

As Sal headed back to me, I noticed Master Cohosaki turn and face me. He was looking at me with an all-knowing smile, even though all I could see were the milky whites of his clouded, aging eyes, eyes that nonetheless glistened with gratification and warmth. I knew no other verbal good-byes were necessary. With that, Cohosaki turned toward the training class and his new salmon students followed.

"Sal," I asked as he swam up to me, "did he just call that other salmon a young Smolts? And what was that noise you made to Master Cohosaki?"

"What do you mean?" he answered bluntly, as if I had caught him off guard. "It was just a little inside joke," he replied. "And that noise, well, I did not think you would hear it, but I should have anticipated your keener senses by now. Either way, that was salmonese," he said defensively.

"What did you say? Salmonese?" I asked with a slight grin.

"Yes, young Smolts, think about it. Do you really think we salmon speak English down here all the time?" Sal asked pointedly. "We are using English with you to make your training more seamless. I did not want you to have to learn a whole new language before your training. You are now trained to the point that your senses are picking up tones and vibrations and subtleties that you have never felt before. I wish upon you the knowledge and skill to use them when you most need them," he added.

"Wow!" I blurted. "A whole new language. But what did those sounds mean?" I asked eagerly.

"Oh, you mean *squuii ubieii yiie leee bweeee,*" as he repeated the new salmonese to me. "It means, 'Until we meet again my friend, Swim strong, swim free."

"That is sooo cool," I answered back, "but what does—?"

Sal abruptly cut me off. "Enough questions. We have to move on. There is a storm ahead!" As he said that, I could feel it. I could feel the change in the pressure of the water and the air. I sensed the animals around me starting to prepare. I liked my newly developed senses, and we looked for a safe place to go.

"We must get in position to weather the storm; then we will continue onward," Sal explained.

"Yes, but I have to tell you, Sal, this is all amazing! The parallels between the salmon's world and my world are both limitless and—"

"Okay, enough!" Sal said in a voice commanding me to be silent. "I know what you feel, and it is a good thing. But we have an arduous journey ahead." With some hesitation, he added, "But we will swim it anyway," as he gave me a reassuring wink.

I knew to be quiet now, because I could feel the water flow against us increasing in force. My new senses were picking up danger signals. My eyes became ever more alert as Sal continued to talk. He commented on how I looked bigger and stronger and how I swam with more confidence and precision. Even so, he still dwarfed me. I let out a small laugh as I imagined I looked like a PT boat being escorted by a battleship as we swam toward safety.

We headed upstream past the training area into a wider

stretch of water. Sal instructed me to use the terrain to my advantage and showed me the safe spots to seek refuge when a storm blows through. He explained, "Sometimes you have to give one hundred percent just to maintain where you are, but when things clear up, you move forward. Let the opposing forces become an afterthought as you become one with the environment around you."

It was all making sense to me now as Sal and I swam behind a huge log just in time to let some large debris rush by. As we hovered behind the log, the rain was pounding the surface above. "The water forces are very strong!" Sal yelled over the increasing roar of the water, "so keep a lookout!"

"Uhhh . . . okay!" I responded nervously as I hunkered down and tried to protect myself from the ever-menacing pieces of debris surging downriver and causing erosion.

Between the many branches and debris smashing past me, I spotted what looked like a dead salmon floating by.

Sal noticed the salmon and was jolted into attention. The surging current was rushing the stunned salmon toward a pair of jagged, monolithic boulders. The swirling vortex between the boulders would easily grind the salmon into shreds like a blender, I worried.

Sal set out at a speed I could not comprehend and was on the dazed fish in a heartbeat. He rushed at him from behind and, just as the salmon was entering the raging death trap, my mentor grabbed him with his massive jaws and quickly turned around, fighting hard to head back to our cover.

The force of the water was unrelenting as Sal fought the foaming current while holding the twenty-pound fish in his mouth. I made a move to help him, but I could see from Sal's expression that he did not want me in harm's way. He stalled for a brief moment as the current hurtled down some sticks and branches at him. But he kicked hard at just the right moment and broke free into the calmer water. I swam out toward them and helped Sal bring the other salmon to the safety of the log.

The injured salmon came to and was surprised to be alive. Sal tended to his wounds, and I looked around for some grubs for him. After finding a nice-sized nymph, I brought it up to him.

The salmon took the food and thanked us profusely. "How can I repay you?" he asked. Sal would have none of it. "A simple *thank you* is enough," Sal said. As soon as the rain subsided and the water cleared, the recovered salmon took off to continue his journey after thanking us again.

I knew I shouldn't ask, but I had to know: "Sal, why did you risk your life to save that salmon? I mean, you could have gotten killed! That water was dangerous. If you two had been washed into that rocky whirlpool, it would have been the end." I rambled on and on, "You did not even know him, or how hurt he was, or—"

"Smolts!" Sal interrupted me, annoyed. "I feel your concern for my safety. I weighed the risk before I decided to help. I want you to understand that we are here to help one another. The phrase *be your own salmon* does not mean be concerned only with yourself. When you are able, always help your fellow salmon. Do not ask for a reward. Let the reward be that you did the right thing. Besides, humanity is not an option; it is a necessity," he lectured.

"I want to show you something. Come!" he ordered after the water calmed down a little. We burst upstream at a fast clip. We swam though large, quiet, deep pools, sometimes resting and other times just keeping an even pace. I followed Sal as we continued farther upriver. I could see the surface terrain changing as we made our way from fairly flat land to the foothills. Sal turned to ask me, "What do you see and feel?"

"Okay, here goes," I said confidently. "I feel I am ready for my journey. I have trained hard, and I know to think ahead and to stay positive. If I fail, I will persevere through learning, determination, and effort. I will give one hundred percent and try to help my fellow man." I tried to think of all my lessons.

"Good . . . what else?" Sal said.

"What else? Uh, no guarantees. And use the percentages."

"Okay, enough!" Sal said, ordering me to stop. "Tell me what you have seen so far since we left the log."

Hmm, is this a trick question? No, he has to be serious, I thought. I gave it my best shot. "I saw the side of you, Sal, as we swam upriver, and I saw some other salmon. There was a big rock outcropping. And I saw a crawfish, but he ducked away before I—"

"Enough! Did you not see how the sun reflected off the exposed bedrock in the last set of falls, causing a rainbow of colors to shimmer as the water rushed over? Did you not notice how, as you jumped, you could see the snow-capped mountains, the fabulous towering pine trees?" He pressed at me. "And how the sun shines through the water and lights up the granite river bottom? What about how when it rains, a thousand little circles form above us that quickly blend into each other? What I am telling you, young Smolts, is to take deep breaths . . . and *enjoy the journey*!"

Sal added, "The reasons for living involve all the things that you said you have learned and more. But I want you to understand this, Smolts—*it is all for nothing unless you enjoy yourself responsibly on your journey.*"

"Enjoy myself responsibly?" I asked, not really understanding what he meant.

"Yes, we are all obligated to enjoy the journey," Sal repeated. "Much of that involves loving what you choose to do for a living and whom you choose as your friends and companions. That is why I want you to know that the great river works in all fairness. The river is wide. The river brings down a multitude of things, good and bad and everything in between, all coming down at different times and different speeds. Are you following me?" he asked as I nodded my head.

"The river is normally most clear toward the middle or the main part of the stream," Sal continued in his best professorial tone. "Now, as we work our way toward the edge of the river, that is where most of the danger is. There are many salmon that live *on the edge,* just as there are many humans who do so. For example, hard criminals and drug abusers live too close to the edge—people who lie and cheat and harm their fellow man. These people are like the salmon that want to live on the edge of the river. They do not understand that the edge is where the majority of the salmon get hurt and killed.

"For salmon, it is easy to see why," Sal continued. "The closer to shore, the more we are exposed to predators such as men and bears. Or we may take the wrong turn in the river and never be able to find our way back to the main stream. The edge has hazards and traps, back eddies that could snare a salmon and cause him to be caught in the same cesspool for years.

"If that ever happens to you, you must fight with all your heart and mind to escape," Sal warned. "Do you understand?" he pressed anxiously.

"That will never happen to me, Sal," I replied.

"Truthfulness is the foundation of personal growth," Sal interrupted. "It is a long life you will lead, young Smolts. Do not ever think that you will never be tempted to swim to the edge every once in a while. When you do, be on guard. If you ever feel the forces of the dirty water moving against you, or the water staining your skin, swim and fight to escape with everything you have. And don't always think that you are the one who can swim in the dirty water and wash completely free of the stain that it leaves on you," he said.

"What do you mean by that?" I asked.

"I mean, not all stains can be washed off, so be very careful where you swim," Sal warned. "Some humans are in an internal or mental jail because they have done things that are unacceptable in any world. Those stains follow them, even if they swim in the clear water and try to wash them off. The stain eventually will rot their soul and they will die, even if their flesh is intact."

"So you're saying that you never really get away with a sin, even if you physically never face punishment for it," I responded.

"Yes! You see, down here we have no jails, but justice is still served by this method. You have jails in your world, but your man serves the same fate of the salmon even if he is not caught, or if he is caught and set free. He is still guilty. He will suffer the same fate," Sal said with supreme confidence.

"Swimming in the clear water is the best way," he added abruptly.

Then Sal calmed down and began to tell me why he was being so serious. He explained that he had family members who had been caught up with polluted waters infested with human waste and garbage—the salmon equivalent of heavy drug use. It took years for them to break free. Even though it is never too late to start moving up the great river again, he suggested, you do not want to set yourself back and lose out on a major part of the great journey. He told me that once the water runs by you, it runs by you . . . and it is gone.

So simple, but so profound, I thought. Once time has passed, that's it. *Another reason salmon always look ahead,* I surmised.

I thought back to those salmon that had given me a false warning and didn't try to make it up the falls. Who knows how long they stayed in that one place on the great river before they mustered the courage to break free.

Sal repeated that the cleaner water is in the middle of the river, and he had a saying about it. "Clean water in, clean water out. Or, in a human's case, clean air in, clean air out."

The phrase is supposed to mean that if you lead a clean life, good things will happen to you. It made sense. The water at the edge is always dirtier and, when you swim there, you can taste the filth in your body. When I drank and smoked too much, I had experiences where my body gave me similar warnings.

Sal said all this knowing I would still have to experience the river of life. He just wanted to make it easier for me to navigate its crazy waterways and maybe save me from swimming into muddy water.

I began to feel at ease as I absorbed what Sal was saying. I began having an explosion of feelings and sensations that I had never experienced before. This strange experience opened up new vistas of learning and achievement for me. I remembered what Sal had told me earlier, "You must learn to be comfortable *outside your comfort zone.*" And I was learning and maturing and becoming stronger by the minute.

I began to look around more, as Sal urged, as we continued swimming. The beauty of it all was enchanting. Even the smooth river gravel that lined the rumpled river bottom had its own beauty. The sunlight reflected the various colors of the tumbling pebbles and the settled rocks. I followed the flow of the water as it rolled between a set of large boulders. From below the waterline, I could behold the amazing sight of the water plunging downstream. It caused a swirl of colors that rivaled the wildest kaleidoscope one could ever pick up.

Suddenly, something caught my eye. I glanced down and noticed gold nuggets lining a huge crevice that crossed the river below me.

"Holy smokes, Sal. It's gold!" I shouted. I broke away from him and dove straight down. I swam to the crevice and spotted ounces of beautiful, glimmering gold nuggets that had wedged in the bedrock and had become exposed by the recent heavy water flow.

"We'll be rich!" I said to him as I tried to nudge a nugget out with my nose.

"Ouch!" I yelled, scraping my snout on a sharp piece of rock.

"What are you doing, you crazy young fish?" Sal yelled to me. "Get back up here."

But, Sal!" I stammered. "There's gold down here!"

"Gold?" Sal answered quizzically. "Those are just shiny rocks."

"What?" I shot back as if he were joking. "What are you talking about? There must be thousands of dollars' worth of gold down here!"

"Hey, they are only shiny rocks to us, young Smolts," he responded. "Think about it," he said dispassionately. "Down here, we have no physical possessions," he added. "I guess that is the equivalent of being naked in your world."

I had to laugh, because I had never thought of it that way.

"Therefore, our happiness is determined not by physical possessions, but by our spirits, our hearts, our souls . . . our levels of *salmonality* . . . what you call humanity," he said in that tone that was now so familiar.

I suddenly realized what he meant. Gold and money have no meaning to the salmon.

"I think I understand, Sal," I told him as I pondered his salmon way of thinking.

"Don't think! Feel... It's our journey in the great river of life, and the way that we swim it, the courses that we take, and the other salmon we choose to swim with that constitutes our passion, our love, our life! That is *our* gold," Sal said with a rare display of passion and finality. "As it should be yours," he added in a quiet tone. "Besides, many a human has drowned with his pockets stuffed with gold. That is why those gold nuggets down there are merely shiny rocks," he concluded.

13

Foot by Foot up Lilliput Trail

Shiny rocks or not, it would be nice to have some, I was thinking when Sal suddenly informed me that we were heading for the last phase of my training. After that, I recalled with some trepidation, would be the Test of the Great Waterfall. But I knew I was ready.

As we headed upriver, Sal began to reveal some of the things I would encounter on my journey through life. "Young Smolts, the river will throw all sorts of things at you on your journey, so you don't want to anticipate the outcome. Let nature take its course, because just at the moment when you need them, these lessons you have learned will be there to support you. The outcome is never the focus. Always, the next activity is your focus," he reminded me.

"Always remember," Sal added, "the river flow is constant, and so must be your effort. Your journey may have periods of calm, clear water, and then all of a sudden it will be full of bends and curves filled with muddy, filthy water," he explained. "Sometimes the path will be clear, and sometimes it will be dark and full of danger. You will eventually encounter all kinds of things in the river of life. Do not take winding detours. What you must do is stay centered in the stream of life; pick a pure, clean course and stick with it. As I explained earlier, the things that do the most harm come down on those living on the edge. Learn to be your own best friend," Sal said.

"My own best friend? What do you mean?" I asked in all innocence.

"I mean, when times get tough and you need advice, turn to yourself. Ask yourself, 'What would my best friend do if he was giving me the best advice he could?' Most times, it will be the right advice. Do you understand?" he asked.

"I understand," I replied. "I remember the times I could have used better advice, Sal. Looking back, I wish I had made some better choices. And I wish—"

"Smolts!" Sal interrupted. "The past is like the water that flows downstream. Even if the water does not seem to be moving at times, it all eventually flows behind us. It will never be ahead of us again. Let your past mistakes be like the water and let it flow behind you. That is why it is so important to keep your nose pointed upstream, as I have said before," Sal said curtly. "The water flow is a constant. So must be your effort. And wishes? Let's just say that if wishes were seahorses, we would all be riding, would we not, young Smolts?" Sal added laughing.

If wishes were seahorses . . . we would all be riding? I pondered. "Hmmm, I think I get it. If we had a seahorse for every wish we made, then we could ride the seahorse and not have to swim."

Sal nodded in approval.

As we swam along, my senses became excited. I began to feel a force ahead, and then I heard an increasing roar. "Is that the waterfall for my final test?" I asked Sal.

"No, that is a smaller set of falls, the falls where you will practice," Sal answered. "You see, one of the final lessons is a very important one. You will learn perseverance and bravery . . . and *character*. Coupled with your newfound knowledge, your physical strength, and your positive mental attitude, your chances of success will be increased."

Sal continued to explain that unrelenting persistence was a vital part of the journey of life and that giving up was not an option.

"I want you to see something," Sal urged as he swam toward the surface.

I had already noticed the river starting to move faster and become narrower, and when I put my head above the water, I could see why. We were past the flatlands and deep inside a long canyon.

"This is not my old river," I observed.

"Oh, rivers are rivers," Sal replied. "This one is a bit more wild than what you are used to. But what fun it would be to make your ultimate challenge a swim up that human-tangled waterway you call the American River, eh, Smolts?" he laughed.

The first things that caught my eyes as I came up out of the water were massive granite boulders that looked like miniature half domes from Yosemite Valley. They towered above my tiny fish head as I peered from the river's surface.

After ducking under to catch a quick breath, I resurfaced and noticed countless towering sugar pines and redwoods growing on the steep banks above the many boulders and rocks lining the river. The mammoth trees rose over the bank like sentinels guarding the river. The sides of the canyon rose steeply, taking the trees up hundreds of yards on each side. I felt as small as a river pebble.

Straining my eyes, I could see thick manzanita bushes that formed a dark green layer beyond the great pines and stretched along the sides of the canyon as far as the eye could see. It seemed like an impenetrable boarder of tangled branches and leaves. Beyond that was a strip of rolling land pockmarked by giant eruptions of jagged shale and boulders that served as monuments to the massive upheavals that formed the canyon millions of years ago.

On the right side of the river, a steep long ridge totally devoid of life bore a faint reflection from the fading sun. The barren terrain finished off the mountain ridge. The ponderosa pines stood as lookouts to the valley and river below.

"Wow. It must be five thousand feet elevation at the top," I told Sal excitedly.

"Six thousand, one hundred twenty-six, to be exact," Sal explained, as I again wondered how this fish knew so much about things only humans generally care to quantify. "This area is called Yuba Canyon. One trail, in and out. It is known as Lilliput Trail because we are in the land of the great trees. The trees rise along with the canyon and make anything look infinitely small in comparison," he explained. "Do you see those men on the trail?"

"What men?" I asked, as I could barely see a trail, much less men. Then I noticed a neatly cleaned campsite that had just been abandoned. I looked for a trail and saw its beginning as it meandered into tall pines and disappeared into the thick manzanita.

"I see the trail, Sal, but it disappears," I told him.

"Look again," Sal directed.

So my eyes followed the trail into the brush until it stopped. A couple hundred yards beyond that, above the manzanita, the trail broke out and continued up the steep canyon side. It snaked around large boulders and shrubs and eventually led to an extra steep area near the top. "I see it, Sal," I told him.

"Good. Now do you see the men hiking?" Sal asked me.

I squinted to see and felt it would surely be nice to have some binoculars right about now. Sal tried to point out the men. I strained and could barely see some tiny ant-like figures slowly moving up the trail.

"I think I see them," I declared. "They seem to be stopping and starting all at different times," I told him.

"Yes. It is good that you see these men, young Smolts. They have to park their vehicles up on that ridge and hike down. It is the only way to access this part of the river. I happen to know that these same men have been hiking down the canyon and back up every year for the last twenty-five years," Sal recalled.

"You have got to be kidding," I answered. "Why would they do that? It looks like such hard labor hiking up the mountain. They've got to be crazy; plus, it looks like they will never make it to the top."

"As for why they do it," Sal replied, "they catch a few fish, but they release most of them. They jump off a place they call 'the big rock' into the freezing water as an initiation to the campsite. They swim, they yell as loud as they want, they stare at the Milky Way and the billions of stars at night, and they look for shooting stars. They sit around a campfire at night, mesmerized by the flames that dance off the river's reflections. One of them sings like a jukebox, the others adding a sound or two. It is quite a sight," Sal said, as if he had witnessed it himself over the years.

"I believe it is because they love camping at a spot where very few can camp," he added. "They are enjoying their journey through life in the company of friends," Sal said quietly, his voice trailing off somewhat. "That is one of the reasons I pointed them out." A quiet moment passed, and Sal snapped back to full attention.

"But there is a more important reason I showed them to you, Smolts. What do you see them doing?" he asked expectantly.

"They are struggling to get to the top of the ridge," I said. "It looks like they started hiking up as a group, but they have become separated. And they are resting at different intervals."

"Good, good. I was hoping we would see them that way," Sal said. "You see, they are not all in sufficient physical shape to climb the mountain without resting. They are weekend warriors." I understood.

"But they are so determined to make it to the top," I observed.

"Yes, so what are their options?" Sal replied.

"Options . . . what do you mean, options?" I asked quizzically. "They are out in the middle of nowhere. If they don't get back to their vehicle, they will never get home. They have no options."

"Exactly," Sal replied. "They learned on the first trip down the valley that once you have chosen to take the journey, you do not have the option of turning back. You see, on the way down it is relatively easy. They have fresh legs and they are hiking down. For three days they hike around the valley floor, fishing and exploring. When it is time to go, they are physically beat up, but they have to hike up to their vehicles three miles above. They found that after the first hundred yards up the trail, they were in huge trouble physically. They knew the only thing that was going to get them back to the top was to build the mental strength to make it. They learned the one-step-at-a-time rule . . . or, in our case, one waterfall at a time," Sal observed.

"Is that why they are all stopping at different times?" I asked Sal.

"Yes!" he replied. "They all have a different level of mental and physical fitness to which they can push their bodies. Once they reach it, they stop and rest. After they have rested, they get up and forge ahead until they can go no farther."

I imagined what the shock must be as they initially put on their heavy backpacks and start hiking up the trail. Manzanita grows thick. I could only imagine their struggle to fight through it all, much like a salmon working his way up a tough waterfall.

Hmmm, this Sal is a smart one, I thought, as I saw another man rest, then get up and hike another thirty feet, then stop and rest again.

"They are doing what they have to do to reach the goal . . . the top," Sal asserted in that mentor-like tone of his. "Resting is okay because it is part of the pace you need to make it to the top."

Sal added, "Having a path you are committed to is one thing, but having the persistence to keep getting up and going farther is another. There's an old saying—'your longitude and your latitude often depends on your attitude.' You should remember that one, Smolts."

Your longitude and latitude. I tossed it around in my mind. I realized the lesson is simple: where you are on the trail, and probably in life, often depends on your attitude.

As we plunged back underwater, Sal let me know it was time to move on. He asked me to hurry because the waterfall ahead was at full fury—*just as he wanted it,* I might add. When I heard the roar, I knew and felt what he meant by full fury.

I noticed the river bottom grow shallow and rocky as the water flow picked up speed. Things were happening fast, as Sal moved me into position for a run up what looked like a twenty-foot waterfall.

"Sal, uh, do you think I am ready?" I asked tentatively. "How high is it, anyway?" My heart began to beat faster with every wave of the river crashing against us.

"I know you are ready, young Smolts." Sal replied in a calm, reassuring voice. "This is about a fifteen-foot waterfall. You will swim to the top. I will watch from here. Remember, this is no waterfall for a swimmer," Sal warned.

I thought of what Kevin Martin, one of the top finance managers at work, would always say as his manager continued to push his monthly sales goals higher: this is no hill for a climber. I figured it meant the same thing, and I was determined to forge ahead. But even with all my training, my stomach was in knots.

"Sal, I'm a little rattled," I finally spit out, wondering if I would throw up or regurgitate or whatever salmon do under stress.

"Nervousness is okay," Sal assured me. "It is the mind's way of getting yourself going. Nervousness lets you know you are alive. Use what you have learned, young Smolts, and you will do fine."

Okay, I thought. My mind raced through all of my lessons.

Be prepared. Don't think, feel. Persistence, flow, use numbers, think positive . . . be the water.

Holy river water, there's a lot to remember, I thought as Sal directed me toward the starting area. A little panic was setting in, I must admit.

"Be aware!" Sal shouted, as I got ready for my run.

"Be aware? Be aware?"

I thought of one of Master Cohosaki's lessons: "Awareness is without choice, without demand, without anxiety. In that state of mind, perception becomes reality. With perception you will feel the path to your success. The ice melts and becomes the water. It becomes the river. Be the water, young Smolts."

Suddenly my anxious mind eased as my senses heightened. I let the water run through my open mouth and gills. Without thinking or pondering, I let the water flow in and around me. I was *feeling.* My senses took over and guided me forward. The course was the vision ahead. I had become part of the river. I was in my zone.

"Now!" I commanded myself as my senses seemed to burst. My tail kicked rapidly into motion. My sleek silver body raced toward the falls. I chose the left side because I could tell it was the best way up. I was surprised at how easily I was soaring higher and higher. As I floated over the top, I was in a state of euphoria unlike anything I had felt in years. I had made it!

"Sal, I made it! I made it!" I yelled as the river fell below me. I barely had those words out when a large wave crashed into my side and sent me tumbling backward.

"Whooaaah!" I screamed. Bad memories flashed before me as I splashed back into the pool below. I lingered in the turbulence for a few seconds and then quickly regained my composure. I spun around looking for notes of sympathy and support from my mentor, but Sal was almost doubled over in laughter.

"What the heck was that all about?" I demanded as I swam up to Sal.

"You failed to swim through the finish line. That is what happened," Sal explained calmly, his mirth now mercifully in check. You did great until you chose to celebrate at the top," he added.

"But I reached my goal," I told Sal. "What did I do wrong?"

"Do not have *a goal*. Have goals!" Sal shouted. "Smolts, always run *through* your goal line. You never know what is going to hit you when you get to the top. In a sense, life is a game. As a baseball player runs out every play and a football player runs through the end zone or a golfer plays through his last shot, they all stick with their routine throughout their game. In your case, sell through the end of the month. Let your momentum carry you into the next month! Does that make sense?" Sal asked.

"It sure does," I answered as I licked my mental wounds and circled around to face the raging waterfall again.

"Now, we will make a few more runs here," Sal urged, "and then we will head up to a resting area to get ready for the Big Ultimate Test."

"You make it sound so hard," I replied. "So what is this Big Ultimate Test?"

"Oh, you will soon find out," Sal said in a monotone. "Find out soon, you will."

I knew it would be of no use to ask him to explain further.

I made a few more runs with ease, swimming through each set of falls as if they were connected. These successes gave me confidence that the twenty-foot falls for the big test would be no problem.

Then, just as I was about to swim back around for another run, Sal suddenly announced, "We are done. It's time to head upstream a bit." His massive body turned sharply as he took off. I followed, still a bit winded from the day of exercise but feeling good.

Sal and I made good time as we headed up an easy stretch of water that he said lay a mile or so below the test area.

"We will rest here," Sal said. We slowed and set up behind a large boulder. "Eat. You need to nourish your body. Gather your thoughts. Rest, young Smolts," he said in an almost fatherly way. "We will go in about an hour."

"Thanks, Sal," I replied in admiration. I settled down and tried to rest. It wasn't easy because I was nervous, but I remained confident about the test ahead.

I began to think of this strange journey with Sal and his friends and the lessons they had taught me. I was very thankful for everything. When I returned to the surface as a human, I knew I would surely keep my agreement with Sal and release him. My mind wandered more as I pondered my surroundings. The river below the surface was mesmerizing. I noticed and sensed all types of wildlife around me. As the sun broke from behind the clouds and showered the pool with brilliance, I suddenly blurted a question to Sal.

"Sal, is there a god in your salmon world?"

"What is that you ask, young Smolts?" he replied. "You mean a supreme being? Smolts, look around you," he commanded as his eyes swept across the beauty of the underwater garden that surrounded us. "We live in a bewildering magnificence down here. Does that question need to be asked?"

Then Sal hesitated. "Do *we* have a god? Do *you* have a god?" he asked, not expecting an answer. "I wondered when you would finally ask me the eternal question," Sal added. "All I can do is tell you, young Smolts, that you must answer that question yourself. But before you do, look around you. See how nature has connected every living creature. Men and animals all depend on the great waterways that feed the land. The sun, the moon, the stars, the earth . . . they all work in cadence together to form one march of life," Sal continued. "All have been around for millions of years before you. When a salmon swims the great oceans, he eats and drinks from areas of the earth that you never see. Humans consume fruits, fish, animals, and vegetables from all regions of the earth where animals and people lived centuries before. What I am trying to tell you is that every living animal is connected to each other in some mystical way." Sal was in his most pontifical state.

"A god? The answer comes from one's soul and cannot be decided by another," Sal asserted. "You humans even claim that man evolved from the ocean in a primitive state that crawled onto the shore. So why not make us fish your god?" Sal said with a touch of pride in his voice and a twinkle in his eyes.

I looked around and basked in what Sal was telling me. I breathed his thoughts. Deeply. I absorbed and pondered his wisdom as I hovered almost motionless at the side of this magnificent salmon. "Yes, there is a god, and that god rests inside all living creatures," I said agreeably, as if I was telling Sal something he did not know. "So what is *your* god called?" I asked quietly.

Sal was quiet for a minute, obviously in deep thought. "There is no name for ours," Sal explained. "Even the great Maharishi in your world said, 'There is but one God, but with a hundred names,' and I believe the guru to be a very wise man," Sal asserted.

"Remember, almost all religions work from the same basic principles of goodness, kindness, and humility. The name of the religion or God does not matter," Sal claimed. "What does matter is what you bring to the task of life. Start with making yourself a good salmon—uh, I mean human being. And the rest will take care of itself," Sal concluded.

That Sal is one wise man—uh, I mean salmon. Or is it sal-man? I wondered, as I stared in amazement at the magnificent creature of God that swam by my side. As far as I was concerned, he was more man than most men could ever hope to be.

"Hey Sal, how much do you weigh?" I asked as I returned to more mundane conversation.

"You are not dwelling on that world fishing record again, are you?" Sal asked with a grin.

"Oh, no." I laughed."I was just wondering. You're beyond huge."

"If you must know, I weigh a hundred and three pounds," Sal replied proudly.

"Oh my word. Holy salmon," I repeated. "Easily a world record, easily. Hey, let me ask you something else now, Sal."

"What now, young Smolts?" Sal shot back with a tone that indicated he was tiring of my questioning.

"I have come to realize something, and I want you to tell me the truth," I asked boldly. "When I hooked you, at any time, with your strength, you could have broken free very easily. I had only a thirty-pound line. And don't tell me you could not have escaped. I have seen you do the most incredible things. And when I was drowning, I swear you pulled me out of the deep water. So why did you let me catch you?"

"What?" Sal said in fake astonishment. "I didn't let you—"

"Sal!" I interrupted. "Don't joke with me. I deserve to know. I want to know. Why did you let me catch you? And why are you really training me today?"

Sal's expression changed from surprised to somber. I could feel a flood of memories rushing through his brain. I was about to tell him to forget my question when he turned to me and said, "Deyoung, let's just say I am fulfilling an obligation to an old adversary of mine who became a friend."

I struggled to understand the last of those words as he turned away; for the first time I had heard his voice crack as he spoke. And he had finally called me Deyoung.

Adversary? Friend? I repeated in my head. Then my new senses picked up feelings of remorse and sorrow from Sal, as he slowly swam away, and I knew right then that I would never broach the subject again.

14

FINAL TEST . . . PROMISE KEPT

As Sal and I continued our quest, I took some time to look around and enjoy the surroundings. He mentioned something about a "test of the great waterfall," but I was confident. I was ready. I knew I would successfully pass the test.

"Time to kick some waterfall butt," I boldly declared to Sal. But he seemed a little worried.

"Sal, is everything cool . . . Old Sali-mander?" I asked in a smart-aleck tone.

"Smolts!" Sal said in his Samurai voice, snapping me to instant attention. "It is one thing to be wise. It is another to be a wise ass!" he admonished. "Know the difference. Do not underestimate the Test of the Great Waterfall! It will take all you have learned and more to succeed," he stated vehemently. "Remember, no guarantees!"

"Yes sir," I said in response to the scolding. I was about to tuck my tail and swim away when I heard a distant roar.

"Remember, Smolts, in the vast limitless river ahead, the salmon has but one ally. Himself. Use all your powers, and swim swiftly and with meaning," Sal said as the roar of the turbulent water battered his last few words.

I began to remember some of my many lessons. Swim without

swimming. Use all ways to find the right way. Feel the flow. Be my own salmon ... the lessons were spinning in my head like a top.

I noticed the water pressure surge, followed by a thundering roar coming from the river above us. The water began to stink, and debris starting flying by me like fastballs.

"What the heck is that?" I demanded as I turned to Sal. "Sal? Sal!"

He was gone. Just like that, he was gone.

I could not believe my eyes as I spun 360 degrees, searching the waterway from shore to shore. "Saaaal!" I screamed, to no avail. The surging currents were drowning out my screams.

"Whooaahh!" I screamed as I dodged more debris and what looked like chunks of sushi as it flew down the swift roaring water. Dead salmon, I quickly realized.

"What's happening?" I kept asking. Sal was nowhere to be found, and I realized it was up to me to assess what was happening in my midst.

The water level was higher because of fresh rain, my nose told me. I could taste the rainwater in my system. But what was that other rank smell, I wondered? And where was the twenty-foot waterfall with the pool behind it? What about my test? And what about seeing my master?

My heart was pounding. I decided to risk taking a peek above the water to see what might lie ahead. Rising up to the surface was tough because the water was pushing hard against me. The water line was bubbly from the turbulence, blurring my vision. Slowly my eyes cleared.

"Holy mother of all waterfalls!" That was all I could hear myself mumble. I viewed a half-mile long stretch of twisting, turning, and foaming water. Huge boulders along the left side caused the water to snake left, then right, creating back eddies that resulted in massive whirlpools that sucked in anything that dared float by.

After a long stretch of maybe a hundred yards, I could see several bears hovering along both shores of the large rapids.

"Bears! That's what I smelled back there," I screamed, counting three large black bears and one huge grizzly. They stood like statues on the river's edge and skillfully reached out with their huge jaws to grab salmon by the mouthful as they swam by. As soon as the bears snatched a fish, they would bring it to the shore and rip it apart in seconds. Birds and coyotes finished off whatever scraps were left uneaten.

"Oh no!" I yelled. Sal hadn't warned me about any bears. With that, I noticed a foamy, white veil cascading behind the bears.

"Wow, what a beautiful waterfall. It looks like a bridal veil," I thought for just a split second—until I realized it was the falls I had to swim up.

It was fifty long feet to the top, with caldrons of foaming water that fell to the bottom. Tons of water, running stronger than I had ever seen before. Large branches, lodged between the massive boulders, protruded menacingly from both sides, snagging helpless fish and tearing them to pieces. How am I, Deyoung Smolts, going to get up that humongous waterfall?

"This is not a test! This is an impenetrable barrier between me and my success!" I screamed in horror. "This is not fair! Sal, this is not a fair test! What have you led me into?" I screamed and screamed to no avail, with a voice that was easily drowned out by the crashing water.

Sal? Master Cohosaki? Mommeeeeee? I screamed inside my head, as I searched in desperation for an answer to the monumental task that lay before me.

Regaining my senses, I began to hear Sal's calming voice in my head. "Swim without the burden of thought. Go forward. Be the water."

I had no choice. Not there, not then. *I must go for it!* I chose a path and tore ahead into the raging water. I easily made it up the first part of the falls. I flew into one of the whirlpools and dashed up the other side. I was choosing a path as I pushed onward.

If only I could get to the pool above the old waterfall. I could ask my master what to do. For a split second, I lost concentration. Bad Idea. At that moment I was thrown back by a surge and found myself swirling in the black abyss of a strong whirlpool. The force of the water pinned me against a large half-submerged boulder. I could not move as the relentless force of the water held me tight against the rock. I froze for just a moment, panicked at the thought of being stuck here forever! The water was continuing downstream to my right. If I could just push off the rock a little, I figured, the water flow would take me downstream. "Now!" I screamed as I arched my body and kicked the granite rock with all my might, twisting my frame to let the water catch my scales and gills.

It worked! My body lifted off the rock and the current caught my side, sending me tumbling downstream into the much calmer pool below. I bounced back down the river for a few seconds and quickly recovered my bearings.

My mind began to focus as I fell into a trance-like state. I remembered what Sal once told me: "The salmon has but one ally. Himself."

That's funny, I thought. He also said my best friend was myself.

My mind flashed to the pools of water where Sal had claimed I would see my master. "You will see your master in the reflection of the quiet pools you visited as a youth," he told me.

As a boy, I would scale the large rocks and look down from above and peer into the pools.

See my master in the pool?

I was confused because this was not the same river as the one I grew up on. *Why did Sal say I would see my master? I don't even see any quiet pools!*

That was strange. Most of the time all I saw was a reflection of myself in the pools, caused by the calm water and high afternoon sun. My mind started to race. The only thing I ever saw was a reflection of myself.

The only thing I saw was a reflection of myself. I repeated what I had learned. Be your own best friend. You have but one ally. Look in the mirror. *Be your own salmon.*

Wait a minute . . . I see myself in the reflection. I see myself . . . I will see the master. Can it be? Suddenly I could *feel* the answer!

"I am my own master!" I shouted. "That is what Sal was trying to tell me all along! I am the one I can turn to when the going gets tough. I am the one who will always be there through my life."

I felt a resurgence of pride and happiness, thankful for what I had learned under such a great mentor.

"It is time for me to get it on!" I screamed. I felt an inner power that I had never felt before. "I am the one who will find the path up the river!" I swam out from behind the rock, allowing myself to enjoy the rage of the wild river as it surrounded me and immersed me in its sensations. "This is no waterfall for a swimmer!" I told myself. "Yes . . . *belong*! Wallow in the quagmire. Relish the challenge. Throw yourself into the opposition. Be the water. Don't think—feeeeel."

As if by some born-again force, I could see a clear course before me, a mystically clear path. And at the same time, my body seemed to meld with the river, becoming part of it. The roaring river became a mere trickle in my mind. I could see sticks and debris coming down upon me, and I was avoiding them with ease, even gracefully so. My body knew what to do before it needed to be done. I had no style . . . I was *all* styles. I had no swimming technique; therefore I was *all* techniques. I had no form, so I was formless. Like the water.

My instincts were taking over, just as Sal had said they would, automatically responding to every obstacle I encountered. My actions took little energy, yet yielded maximum efficiency. I took slow deep breaths while imagining a great proud triumph.

I prepared for my mental trigger. It came with a kick of my tail and a snap of my jaw. I was now in my zone, racing upstream through the foaming rapids. My strong and newly trained body dashed up the first stretch of rapids with the ease of a running back avoiding tacklers. I weaved effortlessly around the protruding rocks and branches that blocked my course. The swirling whirlpools that threatened to chew up anything before me now seemed like calm pools, as I guided my sleek silver body upstream.

I dove into the first whirlpool, timing my entry perfectly and working the momentum of the water's swirling action like a spring to push me farther up the river. Rather than fighting the river's power, I was using it. *I had become the water.*

I used the same technique through a series of four large whirlpools. The churning whitewater no longer seemed superior to my precise moves and timing. I easily advanced farther upstream.

But the bears were next. They stood waiting for me, like sentinels guarding the entrance to my tomb. I could feel the water where they were standing, and I judged perfectly the distance they could reach out over the water. I kicked into high gear and flung myself in a perfect line between the ripping claws of the three black bears on one side and the awesome grizzly on the other.

The grizzly's lunge forced me to arch my body sideways in midflight to avoid his razor-sharp claws. As if in slow motion, I could see his massive claw reach toward me, catching nothing but air as I arched gracefully over the empty paws. I didn't have the time to wonder about fate. The bears' empty jaws told the story. I had passed the bear gauntlet, where so many of my brethren had fallen prey.

The force of my escape had thrown me to a large clear pool that lay just below the massive fifty-foot waterfall. The large pool, formed over the ages, was crystal clear and deep and boasted a huge granite peak that stood unmoved by the water swirling about.

I found a place to rest for a while as I contemplated the obstacle before me. I had never tried anything higher than twenty feet before and, for a moment, I wondered how I was going to make it.

"You're not," a voice said.

"Sal! Sal, is that you?" I was hoping as I quickly spun around.

No, it wasn't Sal. It was a small school of salmon gathered at the side of the falls, the same type of salmon that had messed with me when I made my first run up the smaller falls in my initial training with Sal.

"This waterfall is way too hard," one salmon asserted. "Wait until the water slows down and it will be easier," said another. "It can't be done," warned a third.

Dozens of other salmon entered the fray to tell their reasons for not forging ahead.

My mind began to wander. I was losing focus and falling out of my zone. But I took a good look at them. Their skin did not shine like mine. They looked unhealthy and out of shape. They swam around in circles in a state of lethargy.

They were waiting, all right. Waiting too long. I averted my eyes from them and let the roar of the falls drown out their negative voices. "Don't listen to them . . . don't listen to them. I will not listen to any negative voices from the past that have ever told me it can't be done. It not only *can* be done—it *must* be done," I assured myself.

I slipped back into my transcended state of oneness with the water and flashed back to my first meeting with Sal; I thought about how he had obviously let me catch him. How I had resisted his training until he showed me how I could have fun and learn at the same time. He and his friends had given me many different lessons, philosophies, and analogies that I could use. All of this convinced me that Sal would not put me in a position in which I would fail.

The sight was terrible. Other, larger salmon challenging this awesome waterfall were crashing down around me, falling into the whirlpools below. Some were stunned, making themselves easy catches for the bears that had moved down the river.

"Be careful," I told myself. I gathered my energy and set myself into position to make my first, and I hoped my only, run. A path cleared before me and I shot up the waterfall.

I shot up, up, and up the raging waterfall, surging in spurts five feet at a time, as the relentless water pushed against me. I was doing a great job until I got to about twenty-two feet, at which point I could feel my momentum start to slow.

"No!" I shouted. I slowed to almost a standstill in the blinding, foaming water. I flashed on what to do next. I could not go any farther up. The force of the water was pushing me hard, and small bits of wood and dirt were blinding me. At that moment, my mind flashed on Master Cohosaki.

"One who is a seer, eyes never close," he would say. He could see, but he was blind?

Then, almost by some unconscious choice, my eyes closed, like my beloved master Cohosoki. I could not physically see . . . *but I could see*. And as if by some paranormal force, the way became clear.

I sensed a small ledge to my left that created a spot that greatly slowed the water. Without thinking, without seeing, my body suddenly moved into the safe haven. I surely would have fallen backward if I had not done so.

I swam there easily and opened my eyes to see gushes of water crash down around me. The waterfall seemed to have several such spots. If I could make it to two more, I could probably make a run to the top.

But I then decided the better plan was to try to find three

ledges for my final run, giving me enough energy to make it over the top, instead of just to the top.

I rested and gathered my strength. I knew this was where I belonged, in the thick of things, and I loved it! I felt total freedom as my mind instinctively looked for my next entry point into the surging, foaming water.

I could feel that the time was right as I burst up the falls again, this time making it up to a ledge at thirty-five feet. "This is easier," I told myself, "just like the guys on Lilliput trail. I will work my way up, rest when I need, and I will be up and over the waterfall in no time."

"Help! Help!" I heard as I swam, and I looked around for the source of the scream. I glanced up to see a salmon struggling, stuck in a tangle of branches that jutted out of the falling cascade of water.

"Help!" the salmon yelled, his body writhing and twisting in a desperate attempt to free himself from his deadly trap. I recognized him as one of the healthier salmon that had been yelling at me at the bottom of the falls. It looked like he had finally got up the nerve to give the great falls a try.

"How could he have gotten stuck? How is he going to get free? I surely am too busy to help him," I thought. Then I heard Sal's voice: "One never picks the time to be a hero; the time picks you. Humanity is not a choice but a necessity."

"This isn't fair! I can make it to the top," I thought. "I can reach my goal!"

But without further thought, I began looking for ways to free the distressed salmon. In one swift motion, I shot sideways across the falls, kicking with everything I had. I fought the current and kicked up to where to the salmon was wedged into a small cluster of branches that were stuck between some rocks. I flung my body out into the open air and grabbed the main branch that was holding the writhing fish. I hung from the branch with my jaw as the water pounded me. I swayed there for a moment, like a lure dangling from a fishing line. Then, with one great twist, I snapped the branch in two, setting the salmon loose and allowing him to fall back into the foaming water that quickly carried him out of my sight.

He was free! But the momentum of the breaking limb threw me back into the heaviest part of the raging water. I hesitated for a second, thinking I might still make it back to my safety ledge. But it was too late. The fierce water caught my side, plunging me back thirty-five feet down to the pool from which I had just come.

The water rendered me helpless as I plunged toward some jagged rocks. I scraped my barely healed fin on the rocks, reopening the old injury from the first waterfall.

"Oww!" I screamed as I plunged into the large pool at the base of the falls. Stunned, I shot past the falls into the middle of the raging whirlpool that formed the rapids below, spinning twice and then stopping suddenly.

"I've got to get out!" I screamed. With all my strength, I kicked my tail with just enough force to let the water send me whirling around in circles.

"Not this time!" I screamed as I fought the whirlpool's spin. I timed it just right and flung my body upstream back to the base of the large waterfall.

I quickly regained my composure and looked around to assess the damage. The wound was not that bad, but it was bleeding just a little.

"Damn!" I yelled. Had I not stopped to help that other fish, I would probably be up on top already.

That's okay, I thought. My calm returned. *The right thing to do is not a choice. It is simply the right thing to do.* I began to consider what I needed to do to overcome my injury and get back on track.

Clap, flap, clap, flap, clap, flap. I spun around to see the source of the noise. It was a small school of salmon and some other fish. All sorts of underwater creatures had gathered around, even crawfish and little bugs. It was an amazing sight as they swam around me.

At their head was the salmon I had saved from the branch moments ago. He rushed over to greet me with the biggest smile on his face. His expression was surely one of gratitude and respect. "Thank you!" he said, "You are a great salmon. You risked your life to save me. Thank you."

At that point, the salmon joined the other river creatures and they all broke into an applause of flapping fins as the word spread about my daring rescue. I was stunned and did not know what to say. As I swam around to face them, the applause stopped. They grew quiet, as if they expected me to say something.

"You're welcome," I said to the gathering. "I would have done it for anyone, and I hope you would all do the same." That was all I said as I turned to go.

"Wait!" they yelled. "We want to give you a reward for your heroism and bravery.

"Your thank you is reward enough for me. I am just a humble salmon doing the best that I can," I replied.

"Oh, great salmon," one called out. "Give us some words of wisdom for our journey ahead."

"Yes, please, please," they all cheered.

I swam in circles for a moment, pondering what to say to them. The old Deyoung would have bragged to everyone about how he had risked his life to save the other salmon, telling them how hard it was to break the branch while fighting off the raging current. But I remembered one of Master Sal's many lessons. "Be proud without becoming egotistical," he would say. "Let your swimming do the talking for you."

I kicked and turned my battered body to face the admiring creatures and began to speak. "If you want some words of wisdom, I can give you only these: Keep your nose pointed upstream. Give one hundred percent every day. Keep a positive attitude. And try to swim in the clean water. If you do these things, good dreams can come true," I told them. "But there are no guarantees."

I hesitated for a second as if I was done speaking, but in a closing sentence I added, "Oh, and most important of all . . . *be your own salmon*."

With that, I turned and slowly swam away, leaving the crowd in stunned silence as they pondered the words of my humble message.

15

SELF-DISCOVERY

Whew! What an experience, I thought. I tucked into a little cave-like depression on the inside curve of the huge pool the falls created. *I am lucky to be alive,* I thought. Now I have to gather my energy to make the final run.

"Young Smolts . . . young Smolts," called a familiar voice. I sprang instantly from the cave. "That's Deyoung Smolts to you, Sal!" I repeated in jest as I rushed out to meet my friend and mentor. "Sal!" I said excitedly. "What are you doing here? I thought I was going to meet you at the top!"

Sal just swam around me for a second, looking at me like a proud father. "You have passed your test, young Smolts. You have passed it very well."

"I don't understand. I didn't make it to the top. I was just about to make it—" I began to explain.

Sal cut me off. "I know the whole story," Sal said, as I noticed behind him the salmon I had saved.

"This salmon happens to be my brother," Sal said, with a twinkle in his eye. "I saw how you sacrificed your goal to save him. You chose brotherhood over what would have been a temporary victory. That is the true passing of the test," he proclaimed proudly.

"So we are done here," Sal said. And with that, a strange silence enveloped us as the raging water grew instantly calm. I looked around me and suddenly noticed the familiar pool in which I had caught Sal. It was very still, dark, with the full moon sparkling through nearby towering oaks.

"We're home!" I yelled to Sal.

"You don't have to yell, Deyoung. I know where we are," Sal replied. "It's late, and we have to get you back home," he added, as I continued to ponder the sudden end of the final test.

"Oh, man, am I in big trouble!" I exclaimed. I realized I would have some serious explaining to do when I got home. "What am I going to tell my wife?" I asked Sal.

"Oh, tell her the truth. Then she will think you are crazy and divorce you," Sal said with a lighthearted laugh. "Just kidding," he gestured in a mood obviously brighter now that his mentorship was ending and he would soon be free of me . . . or free of a previous obligation.

I began to wonder just how many days or nights had flown by. It seemed as if I was in a dream, flowing from one lesson to another, one day to the next, a wonderful, seamless journey and learning experience transcended only by the awe-inspiring beauty I had passed during this surreal time.

Not really knowing what to expect, I decided to pop to the surface to see what time of day it was. As I rose above the waterline, I found a strange surprise—the full moon was just starting to rise above the same oak it had shown through right before I hit my head. "Sal, " I asked, "was I not gone for days and days?"

"Let us just say the river flows in mysterious ways, Deyoung Smolts, and leave it at that," Sal replied coyly, a big Cheshire cat grin on his face. I then began to worry about the time. How would I explain being gone for so long to everyone?

"We will swim up by the landing spot, and then I will turn you back to a human," Sal declared confidently. "We will then say good-bye from there, and I shall be free and so shall you," he added.

"Then I can be free to move forward with my life," I responded enthusiastically.

"Yes," Sal responded, "but remember what Coho said about freedom. With freedom comes great responsibility, and freedom is like being captain of your own ship. Being the captain, with the freedom to go where you wish, does not mean being able to drift aimlessly among the waves, floating around with no destination or plans. If you do, you will most certainly suffer a shipwreck. Being free means being *the leader of your ship.* You are able to set your own course, to have destinations, to have realistic and achievable goals, but be wise enough to make adjustments to your course as needed."

"Wow. I am still learning . . . and my plan is to never stop," I assured Sal with an adoring smile.

"Oh, you will learn, all right," Sal said. "You will definitely learn."

"Any last words of wisdom?" I jokingly asked Sal, not expecting any answer after the plethora of knowledge that I had already acquired.

"Oh, yes. I do have a couple more things," Sal responded in a nearly frantic tone, as if trying to get in all his last lessons before we parted. "Respect others," he implored. "Do not deceive them. Deception is a sign of disrespect. Always remember that the choices you make determine who you are. Also, your word is your bond; once you lose that you lose your dignity. And never forget that good dreams can come true, but most fantasies stay fantasies. Learn the difference," he said with a trailing finality as we veered toward our parting destination.

Wow! I thought as a flood of emotions swept over me. *Is my journey over?* No, I knew somehow it had just begun. As I contemplated Sal's last words of wisdom, a sudden realization, almost a revelation, came over me. If ever doubt clouded the existence of a divine being, an almighty God, *proof was needed no more!*

Suddenly the flood of emotions subsided and I began to speak. "Sal, I want to thank you for everything," I began to say, fumbling for words that matched his deeds.

"No need!" Sal said. "It was my pleasure. It was my pleasure."

"Is there anything I can do for you, Sal?" I asked innocently.

"No. Nothing is needed. Nothing . . . oh wait, there is one thing, Deyoung."

"What is that?" I asked him, somewhat surprised that he had anything to add at this point.

"When you get back to your world, tell humans that salmon need water to survive. Every year they cut off more water, and the young cannot live without it. They dam up the rivers so we cannot go to our final breeding areas. Sometimes the water we do get is not pure enough to swim in safely. It is full of sewage and pesticides. It kills or deforms our young. It is stopping our life cycle!" he fumed.

"Let humans know," Sal added sternly, "that if the great Almighty cut off their air and restricted their movement, they would not be happy either. You humans need a plan to save the great salmon, one that is realistic and achievable."

Sal continued his rant, his eyes almost bulging with frustration. "Tell people there is an essential oneness in *all* living creatures, yet they continue to treat creatures differently. Tell them that even the weakest elements of nature need protection. If they do not receive it, then all is lost—all—and that could someday include you humans. Being the humans, the most powerful of all species, it is your duty to take care of all living creatures, not just us salmon. If people would start with themselves, make themselves part of the solution, the most devoted could join together. And by using mutual humanity as the common denominator, a human oracle could be formed. By doing so, people and countries could come together to form worldwide solutions," he urged.

I was stunned by what he had asked me. Typical Sal. Nothing for him. Everything for his brothers and all species on this wonderful earth that we are blessed to live on.

"I will tell them, Sal. I will," I assured him, with my voice trailing off at the seriousness of his request.

As the familiar shoreline came into sight, I began to think back over the mystical adventure I had just experienced. This has to be my life epiphany. My everlasting, life-changing moment. The moment that would stay with me—and influence me—all my life.

I knew I had been a personal witness to one of the few places left in this world that is still the way the Almighty made it. And I was trained and taught by, well, simply the best.

Or was this an ephemeral experience, one to be forgotten once I awakened from what had to be a crazy dream?

I just had to ask him. "Sal, will I remember all of this and go on to be a success?"

Sal answered as if he had been expecting the question all along. "Deyoung, the answer you seek, at least in some degree, depends on what you believe," he replied. "Every living creature has an ethereal soul that passes from one generation to another. I have every reason to believe that most of what you have learned can be retained when you pass from a salmon back to a human." He then smiled and motioned his massive head toward the shore.

On what I believe? I pondered that as I slowly followed behind him. I knew that the next step was good-bye . . . and I was not looking forward to it.

An overwhelming sadness engulfed me as we reached the rocky shore. I knew mere words, weak words, now separated us. "Sal, thank you again . . . for everything," I stuttered. "I mean *everything* you have done. You have taught me *more than most men will learn in a lifetime*. You fulfilled your obligation to me and more. And I—"

"That is enough, Mr. Smolts. It is time to go," Sal answered, cutting me off as he had done so often before on this journey.

"Wait! Sal, there is one last thing I want to say."

"What is it, Deyoung?" Sal asked.

"I have grown to love you, and I just wanted you to know . . . I love you, Sal," I proudly said to him, my throat choked with a mix of emotions.

"I know," he said as he turned and looked right at me. "I love you too, Deyoung," he answered. "You would make any father proud to call you son."

For a moment we swam around, neither one of us saying a word. I decided to break up the silence. "Hey, Sal!" I said in an upbeat tone. "Squuii ubieii yiie leee bweeee."

"Hah!" Sal laughed, realizing I had picked up a little of his language. "You are a smart one. Now you swim hard, swim free, Deyoung. I am proud to call you my student, my friend."

Then it was his turn to speak in salmonese, "Squuii ubieii yiie leee bweeeeeeeeeeeeee."

The *eeeeeeeee* screamed in my head until my mind went blank. At that moment, I felt the sudden rush of cold night air, and my head began first to spin, then go instantly clear.

"Woohooooooo! It's fricking cold!" I heard myself shouting as I stood in the evening air shaking like a wet dog. I realized I was no longer swimming but was standing in knee-deep water by a boulder under the moonlight . . . with a five-foot-long salmon attached to my stringer.

"Man, oooh, man," I blurted as my head pounded with the memories and images and the knowledge of what just happened to me. "I remember it all . . . *all* . . . I remember it all!" I now spoke the language of nature. I was as close to the heart of this world as one human could ever get. I stood there, amazed and somewhat bewildered, and I began to cry.

I stood there sobbing, my tear-clouded eyes staring up at the now brilliant glowing moon. As my eyes slowly cleared, I noticed a huge perfect ring circling the moon. I knew it was an ice-ring from the cold air and moisture left over from the receding storm.

But it really seemed that mysterious forces had placed a glorious halo around the moon, just for me. The magnificent shimmering ring of light easily filled half the skyline. *Perhaps it's a signal to the end of my magnificent journey,* I pondered as I stood motionless, staring straight at the smiling man on the moon. The heavenly phenomenon seemed to light up my body, and I could feel my strength come back with every absorbed ray of light. For an eternal moment, I stood there—strong and proud—as I basked in God's full glory.

Then a small tug on the stringer reminded me of my promised task ahead.

My senses cleared. Right away, I knew one thing, one thing for sure—I had to let Sal go.

I wiped the water and tears from my face with my free hand as my other hand held the stringer with the priceless Sal on it. I steadied my feet and headed for a slightly deeper area. Slowly, and with utmost care, I pulled the magnificent Salvador, the king of king salmon, out to a nice clear pool to make release easier.

"Can you hear me, Sal?" I said to that magnificent creature.

Sal did not talk. He looked at me with understanding eyes. I could tell his eyes, those eyes I now knew so well, said thank you. The great fish knew, as did I, that our shared experience would be our bond for life.

The full moon helped me see into the dark water as I worked the rope loose and guided it through Sal's mouth. He turned toward me and nodded his head. At that moment he jerked his head up out of the water and spit out a tiny object that I instinctively caught with my right hand. It was too dark to tell what it was, but it felt like the tungsten weight I had put on the line to catch him.

That's cool, I thought. *He wants to give me the weight as a souvenir.* I slipped it into my vest pocket and turned to watch him. He gave me one last good-bye nod and slowly took off toward the falls.

"Good-bye, my master . . . my friend," I whispered as I watched him disappear into dark, rippling water. "Wow. Did I just let that record salmon go?" I asked as I stumbled for the shore.

Of course I had. But that was not the problem. I had to get home.

In my new hurry to reach the shore, as luck would have it, I did not take the same care coming in as I did going out, and I stepped on another slippery rock and lost my balance. "Not again!" I yelled. With no fishing pole in hand this time, I jutted out my arm to brace my fall. But my wet hand slipped on the smooth granite and the momentum sent my elbow and head crashing into the hard rock. I was out cold again.

My mind was fading fast as I slid slowly into the water. My body seemed to give up. *Going back into the water to see Sal?* I wondered, as my body continued to creep perilously closer to the deep pool.

In my grogginess, I sensed a light. Not the moon—this light was small at first and then grew stronger, shattering the darkness. I sensed some splashing . . . and then a voice—a man's voice.

"Are you okay, son? "Are you okay?" the voice repeated, as I felt a strong hand grab my arm and pull me toward the safety of the sandbar.

"Oww!" I yelled as I snapped to and grabbed my pounding head.

"Hold on there, young man. We need to take care of this

wound," the man said. I instantly settled down, trying to open my eyes and adjust to the glare of his light.

I realized that he was not talking about my head but a wound on my elbow that was bleeding.

"How did you get this?" he asked.

I was still very groggy, holding my hand to shield my eyes from the light. After managing to focus, I noticed a younger guy, maybe about thirty or so. He was dressed in fishing gear, but it was old style gear. And the light he was using was not a flashlight but an old gas lantern.

"What's going on?" I asked as I gradually recovered my senses. "Oww! What's wrong with my fin?" I blurted as I bent my elbow. I caught my gaffe. "Ahhh, I mean my elbow," I quickly stammered.

"Well, you tell me," he said, looking at me with a smile. "I come upon you all passed out and half in the water. Your arm looks bad. We need to get that patched up." He whipped out some first-aid gear and sat down to wrap my arm.

"What's your name?" the man asked

"It's Deyoung. Deyoung Smolts," I managed to say. I lay there freezing and shivering. "What's yours?"

"Mine?" he hesitated. "It's Sam ... Sam King," The man replied. "But you can just call me Sam," he offered as he gently washed my injured arm.

"How did you manage to do this?" he asked as he inspected my arm.

"I'm not sure. I stumbled. There was this salmon. A *big* one. And we made a deal. And I got all these lessons. And a big waterfall . . . and a rock . . . and I hurt my fin . . . ahh, I mean my arm." I stuttered. When I realized what I was about to tell him, I stopped. "Well, you wouldn't believe me anyway," I said to Sam.

"Oh, I don't know. I've heard some fishing stories in my day," he said with a little smile on his face. "We'd better get you back to your car," Sam said as he finished wrapping up my arm.

As I gathered up my gear, still groggy, I thought I caught a glimpse of Sam waving out to the water, followed by the faint but familiar sound of a salmon jumping in the distance. I quickly shook it off as my lightheaded condition and looked around for a place to brace my hand so I could push myself up off the soft sand. But my legs went weak. Sam grabbed my shoulder and held me steady.

"Be careful there, Deyoung," he said. He gathered up my pole and creel and slowly lifted me off the sand. "The trail is dark, and I don't have much oil left," Sam said as the lantern flickered. "So we better get moving." He held up the lantern and guided me across the sandbar. We slowly walked down the trail in the dark. I tried to talk to Sam, but he was very vague in his replies.

"Do you live around here?" I asked him.

"I did," he said faintly.

Sam seemed to know his way around the river as we made our way through the thick brush and found the sand path that led back to the cars.

"So, you say you caught a salmon?" Sam asked.

I heard him but hesitated just a second before answering. I figured I could tell him about the salmon. Just not about, well, you know, everything that had happened. After all, would you in my situation? So I went on to say, "Oh, I caught a salmon, all right. And it wasn't just any salmon."

"Oh?" Sam replied, somewhat coyly. I went on to tell him my story about catching the salmon and the fight of my life and how I almost drowned as I fought the mighty beast.

I leaned on him as we walked and talked, groping through the dark riverbank. I noticed that he was a strong man and about my size. He easily supported my weight as we walked down the trail. It seemed so easy to talk to him as we zigzagged up and around old trees and roots on the sandy path back to the cars.

"So how big did you say this fish was?" Sam asked in amazement.

"A hundred and three pounds!" I told him proudly.

"Golly gee," he said. "A hundred and three pounds! That is one darn big fish. You are a lucky man to have caught a salmon like that!"

"Yes, I guess I am. I guess I am," I said. It was just sinking in that I had caught—and then released—that magnificent salmon.

Then Sam said something kind of strange. "You know, Deyoung, catching a salmon like that can teach you a lot about yourself. What did you do with him?"

"Well, I let him go," I said quite sheepishly, because he did not know about the great deal I had made.

He thought for just a second. "That was the right thing to do for such a wonderful creature," he responded. "Now, enough about the salmon. What about you? Are you married?"

I told him about my wonderful wife and boys. He wanted to know their names, James and Michael I announced proudly, as I regained strength and balance.

"That is great," he said, as if he was proud of me.

"And how is your mom?" he asked tentatively.

I was still somewhat groggy from the blow to the head, "Ahh, she's fine, Sam. Fine," I managed to stammer in reply. "But . . . why do you wan to know about my m—?"

"Oh, good. There's the parking lot!" Sam said, interrupting me, loudly enough to distract me from my question.

"We better get you home. It is getting late," he added.

I glanced at my watch. I was stunned. Shocked. Only two hours had gone by since I had caught the big salmon. "Wow. How could all that have happened in that short of a time?" I wondered.

"What did you say, Deyoung?" Sam asked.

"Oh, it's nothing. It's just that no one is going to believe me that I caught such a fabulous salmon, that is—"

"So you have no proof?" Sam asked. We walked toward my car, the only vehicle left in the parking lot.

"No. I have no proof. No, wait! I do have this." I reached into my vest for the tungsten weight that Sal had spit out to me.

Sam brought his lantern closer. I fumbled in my pocket for the weight. I found it among the spinners and small bobbers and grabbed it with my fingers, then I slipped it into my palm and brought it up to the fading lantern.

As we both peered down, I unwrapped my hand. There, to our amazement, lay a gold nugget with just enough quartz to pull sparkles out of the moonlight.

"Wow, that's a nice one!" Sam said.

I was totally shocked as I held the quarter-size nugget between my two fingers. "It's the most beautiful nugget I've ever seen," I declared.

"You are a lucky young man," Sam said. "Where did you find it?"

"Oh, it's a long story. A long story," I told him, still surprised about the nugget.

That Sal, he is a sneaky one, I thought to myself. A large smile grew on my face as the memories of this wondrous night filled my soul.

"You better put that someplace safe," Sam said, snapping me out of my short daydream.

I quickly placed the gold nugget in a pouch where my keys went and tucked it into my pants pocket. "It will be safe there," I said. I gave the nugget a little pat.

My mind was still racing over the events that had unfolded this amazing night, and I began to wonder about this strange man in the old fishing clothes who had helped me out of the river. It was odd, but I felt I owed him much for everything he had done for me. I turned around to face him. "Thank you, Sam," I said. I put my hand out to shake his.

"It is my pleasure, Deyoung. My pleasure."

For the first time I was able to look into his eyes. They were deep blue eyes surrounded by a strong, proud face, and blond hair.

I got a strange feeling about him, but I shook it off, as the cold sent a shiver up my wet spine. I decided it was all nothing. I placed my waders in the trunk. Sam said, "Don't forget these," as he handed me the safety belt for the waders.

"Never go fishing without these again," he said in a deep, concerned voice. Upon hearing those words, I knew I never would forget them again.

"I won't, believe me, I won't," I answered. As I grabbed them and placed them in the trunk, I remembered they had saved my life just a short time ago.

My car was the only one in the parking lot, so I thought Sam might need a ride home. "Hey Sam, do you need a—" I said, glancing around.

But Sam was gone.

"Sam! Sam? Where are you?" I yelled.

I scoured the area under the street lamps, searching for him. I wanted to thank him again and ask him more questions.

I yelled out again, pausing occasionally to listen, but all I could hear was the roar of the river and the buzzing of the night insects. The distant sound of the freeway reminded me of my need to get home.

I stood there confused about the day and the visitors I had met. The memories of this strange night raced through my mind. It was certainly a life-changing moment. All I had to show for the trip was a cut elbow and a small bump on my head, a gold nugget, and enough knowledge to fill a small book. And that was more than enough for me! I smiled and jumped in the car.

When I got home, I told my wife I had stopped to play football in the mud with the guys and had gotten hurt. Tired, really tired,

I hit the sack earlier than usual, praying that I would remember it all when I awoke.

"AND THAT'S WHAT HAPPENED TO me that glorious day, Pete. That is why I am the top salesperson almost every month and will continue to be. I am being my own salmon."

Pete sat mesmerized in his chair, speechless, with a blank gaze. He did not move for what seemed like ten minutes. I stood there, waiting for a response. Any response.

"Pete, are you okay?" I asked, interrupting his befuddlement.

Pete looked at me and blinked once. "Deyoung, that is the most amazing story I have ever heard. I don't even know what to say. I don't know whether to hug you or send you to a doctor," he stammered.

"You say he turned you into a salmon?" Pete asked tentatively. "And you swam to the ocean? And there was a blind salmon? And you visited San Francisco Bay?"

"Yeah, Pete, I know it sounds weird."

"And you learned all those wonderful lessons, and selling techniques, and he gave you a gold nugget. Pete continued.

"Yes! That's why I don't want you to tell anyone."

"Are you kidding me?" he gasped. "No one would believe me anyway. But let me ask you something," Pete said as strange look came on his face, as he began to calm down.

"What?" I replied.

"Deyoung, the guy who helped you to your car . . . what did you say his name was?"

"The guy in the old fishing clothes?" I asked. "It was Sam. Why do you ask?"

"Sam what?" Pete persisted. "What was his last name?"

"Sam King. Why?" I answered, wondering where his curiosity was going.

"Oh, I don't know. That name . . . let me look for something," Pete said. He weakly got up out of his chair and stumbled toward the old storage closet.

"What's up, Pete? What are you looking for?"

Pete did not answer as he made a beeline for the door, grabbed the handle, and swung it open. The dealership was family-owned and had been in this location for more than thirty years. The old closet was full of old Clearance Sale and We'll Take Any Deal signs, plus discarded banners and all the old write-ups and credit applications.

"What is it?" I asked again as Pete moved box after box of old papers and files.

"Help me move these," he finally asked after straining his back.

"What are we looking for, Pete?"

"I just remember seeing something a couple years ago, and I wonder . . . ah, here it is." We cleared the last box that lay against a small, closed door with a sign that read Extra Storage.

"How long has this been here?" I asked, having never seen it before.

"Oh, it was just part of the original storage until they built around it," Pete explained.

"Help me open this," Pete said as we bent down. The door was only about five feet high. We opened the small door slowly, and Pete flipped on the light switch. We peered inside.

"There are just some old boxes in here," I exclaimed. My eyes caught a couple rows of cardboard boxes.

"Yes, that's what we are looking for," Pete said, still confusing me as to why we were in there. The boxes read Receivables 1964, 1965, and 1963. Wholesale, Retail, 1965, 1968.

"That's the one I'm looking for," Pete said as he grabbed it. I couldn't see any writing on the box. He quickly backtracked out of the storage area and left me crouching there.

"Hey, wait for me," I said as I followed Pete out to the sales meeting room.

"What is it?" I asked as he set the box down.

Pete opened the box as I walked around him. I peeked over him and noticed the faded label read Samuel Kingman.

"Who is Samuel Kingman?" I asked Pete. He opened the box.

"Hold on, hold on!" Pete exclaimed, his voice becoming more intense and excited.

Pete opened the box and reached inside. It was filled with plaques. My heart almost stopped as I read, "Sam King—Salesman of the Year, 1964."

Pete looked at me, also stunned. He pulled out another. "Sam King—Salesman of the Year, 1963."

"Oh my God," I said to Pete. "You don't think . . . do you think this was the Sam King that helped me out?"

"I don't know what to think," Pete said. "I really don't at this point." He stood there, almost shaking.

"It can't be. The guy who helped me was thirty at the most," I assured him. "Hey, Pete, maybe I can meet this Sam Kingman. Is he retired?"

"I don't know," Pete said. "I haven't heard of him, except for this box." He pulled out the last plaque. I noticed that the bottom of the box was lined with an old newspaper.

"These have been here a long time," Pete said. I reached down and carefully peeled the brittle paper from off the bottom of the box. It felt almost warm to the touch. I held it in the light and wondered why old newspapers were in there. It was old, like the plaques, and it was a front page. Pete noticed I had it and came over to look at it with me. I carefully unfolded it and spread it out on the table—*The Sacramento Bee,* October 8, 1966.

The front headline mentioned the Vietnam War and listed some casualties. We both continued reading, getting a kick out of the old news. Almost at the same time, Pete and I stopped dead in our tracks as we noticed—then read—the same article:

> Local Veteran and Automobile Salesperson Dies in Tragic River Accident
>
> Samuel Kingman, better known as Sam King to his many friends and customers, died yesterday in a tragic accident while fishing in the American River. Yesterday evening, divers found the body of Mr. Kingman in a deep-water depression, near a popular fishing spot below the dangerous Great Nomlas Rapids near the Discovery Park Recreation Area.
>
> A witness on the other side of the river was unable to help. He reports that he saw Mr. Kingman fishing around 6:00 PM. The witness said it appeared Kingman was fighting a salmon as he worked his way down the river. At one point, Mr. Kingman was waist deep in the water and the witness claimed Kingman slipped or fell into a hole on the river bottom. The bystander reported seeing Mr. Kingman go below the surface, and that's when he called authorities. Divers reported that they found his body in ten feet of water. His waders had filled with water, causing drowning.
>
> Game Warden John Henry stated, "All fisherman should be using a safety belt with their waders. It appeared Mr. Kingman was fighting a fish, because he was found with a pole and broken line. He truly died doing what he loved.
>
> Mr. Kingman, a military veteran who was recently married, was looking forward to the birth of his first child.

As I read the article I began to shake and my knees began to weaken. As I read the last few lines, my legs finally buckled.

Leaning against the table was the only thing that stopped me from falling on the floor. Pete grabbed my arm and held me steady. I continued to read:

> He leaves behind his many friends and family plus his beloved wife, Fusako Kingman, whom he met while stationed in Japan during his military service. Funeral services will be announced.

My mind began to spin out of control. I had heard the Kingman name before, years ago when I was a very young boy. I could not place it until now.

"Are you okay?" Pete asked, while holding me steady. "What is it? I know the guy has a similar name, but maybe it's just, you know, coincidence."

"No, Pete! You don't understand," I almost shouted, as I lay there slumped against the table, shaking and shivering profusely. "Fusako is my mom's name, and now I remember where I've heard the Kingman name before. Kingman was her last name from her first marriage. She rarely mentioned it after she remarried when I was eighteen months old. My stepdad is the only father I have ever known, so out of respect for him, I call him Dad and use the Smolts last name, but Kingman is the name on my birth certificate."

My revelation hit Pete like a brick.

"You see, my real dad died before I was born. I . . . I . . . never met my real father . . . until . . ."

Pete braced his free arm on the table and started to sweat. "Oh my God . . . oh my God," he stuttered.

We both stood there staring at the newspaper and the plaques. We slowly turned and hugged each other, both of us fighting back tears. I sobbed and shook in his arms as I realized the magnitude of the story I had just told and the astonishing ending that had fallen upon me.

The story had now come full circle. Sal with the old hook in his jaw. Sam drowning while catching Sal when he was a younger salmon. Sam, after entering Sal's world, somehow got Sal to teach me what he could not, and Sal somehow lived long enough to teach me these important life lessons when I needed them the most. My mind raced with images of Sal, Sam, and Master Cohosaki.

Pete and I both knew something had happened. We just did not know what or how, nor did we know how fully it mattered. We knew we had shared something special, something that may only happen once in a millennium, or once in a lifetime, or never at all.

Pete looked at me with true caring and understanding. I was trying to regain my composure. We both knew we could never say a word to anyone about this. Ever.

"Deyoung, that box, the plaques, the newspaper," he muttered nervously, "it's all yours. Yours to keep," Pete offered. He continued looking at me. "It has been a privilege and an honor to hear your amazing story." Then he stuck his hand out to me for the second time that day. "If you need anything, anything at all—"

"Thank you, Pete. Thank you," I managed to utter as I dried my tears.

Pete turned toward the still-closed door. He hesitated and turned to me. "One last thing, Deyoung," he said.

"What is that?" I asked.

"I understand," Pete said with a sincere, caring look on his face, "that this whole meeting, the story about you, Sal, Sam, the box, and your mom—this is a secret, between you and me only. And you can rest assured that your story will stay between you and me forever." He stood there for a second, then looked me in the eyes, and smiled. "Oh, and until we meet again my friend, swim strong, swim free.

The end.

Epilogue

Rumor has it that Deyoung advanced quickly up the promotional ladder. He also swam confidently through the turbulent river of life, falling back a few times and learning some more hard lessons along the way.

He became a general sales manager and trainer of many top salespeople. He became a good husband and father to his boys. They say he loved his family, fishing, golf, gold prospecting, camping in the mountains, and the ocean. Many called Deyoung their friend.

Deyoung also formed his own nonprofit organization to help the endangered salmon of the area. He enjoyed painting scenes of animals and river life. After hurting his hand gold prospecting, he wrote a best-selling book.

A fairy tale? A crazy dream? Only if you dismiss the validity of everything Sal and Master Cohosaki taught Deyoung and us as we followed him on his fantastic voyage. Only if you do not believe that the right to swim free and choose your own course is born into all of us. Including you, reader.

The story could be true, because the story could be you.

Take the parts out of this book that will help you get to the next level, and the next. If you have friends who need a lift, have them read this book. Tell them to *be your own salmon* and to *swim strong,* because that is what you are doing.

Sal's 25 Lessons for Life

Hundreds of words of wisdom are found in the pages of *Be Your Own Salmon*. You may have highlighted many of them. Sal asked me remind you of the twenty-five you most likely wrote down or highlighted so that you can find them easily in the epilogue. These words can form the new foundation of your character to become the points of strength you can rely upon when the *current is strong* and the *waterfalls* seem insurmountable.

But Sal doesn't know that I added a few more—from the upcoming book, *The Salmon I Am,* in which I will tell of the adventures of Sal and Master Cohosaki's adventures before they met Deyoung.

1. If it is to be, I must believe in me.
2. The water flow is constant, so must be your effort.
3. Your longitude and latitude often depend on your attitude.
4. With closed eyes, one can still see, with a closed mind, one cannot.
5. There is no waterfall too hard for a swimmer.
6. In this vast limitless journey, you have but one ally—yourself.
7. Humanity is not a choice but a necessity.
8. The answer, at least to some degree, depends on what you believe.
9. Swim in the clear water—clean water in, clean water out.
10. Be the message that you send; don't be a hypocrite.
11. Be the water, my friend . . . wallow in the quagmire.

12. The journey ahead is arduous, but you will make it anyway.
13. Doing the right thing is never a choice. Just do it.
14. Good dreams can come true, but most fantasies are meant to stay fantasies.
15. Your choices determine who you are.
16. Let your actions and activities produce your results.
17. When a decision involves your conscience, the decision is yours alone.
18. Plan with your head, but decide with your soul.
19. Use the averages to set your goals—and have goals.
20. A salmon that fails to plan ahead is a salmon that usually winds up dead.
21. Gold is just a shiny rock. The *journey* is your gold.
22. When you are immune to the opinions of others, you will not be the victim you think you are.
23. Always keep your nose pointed upstream.
24. Let you actions speak for you. Humble pie, is good pie.
25. *Squuii ubieii yiie leee bweeee*—Until we meet again my friend, swim strong, swim free.

But most of all . . . *Be Your Own Salmon.*

Thomas S. Dittmar

CPSIA information can be obtained
at www.ICGtesting.com
Printed in the USA
FSOW03n0759080916
24748FS